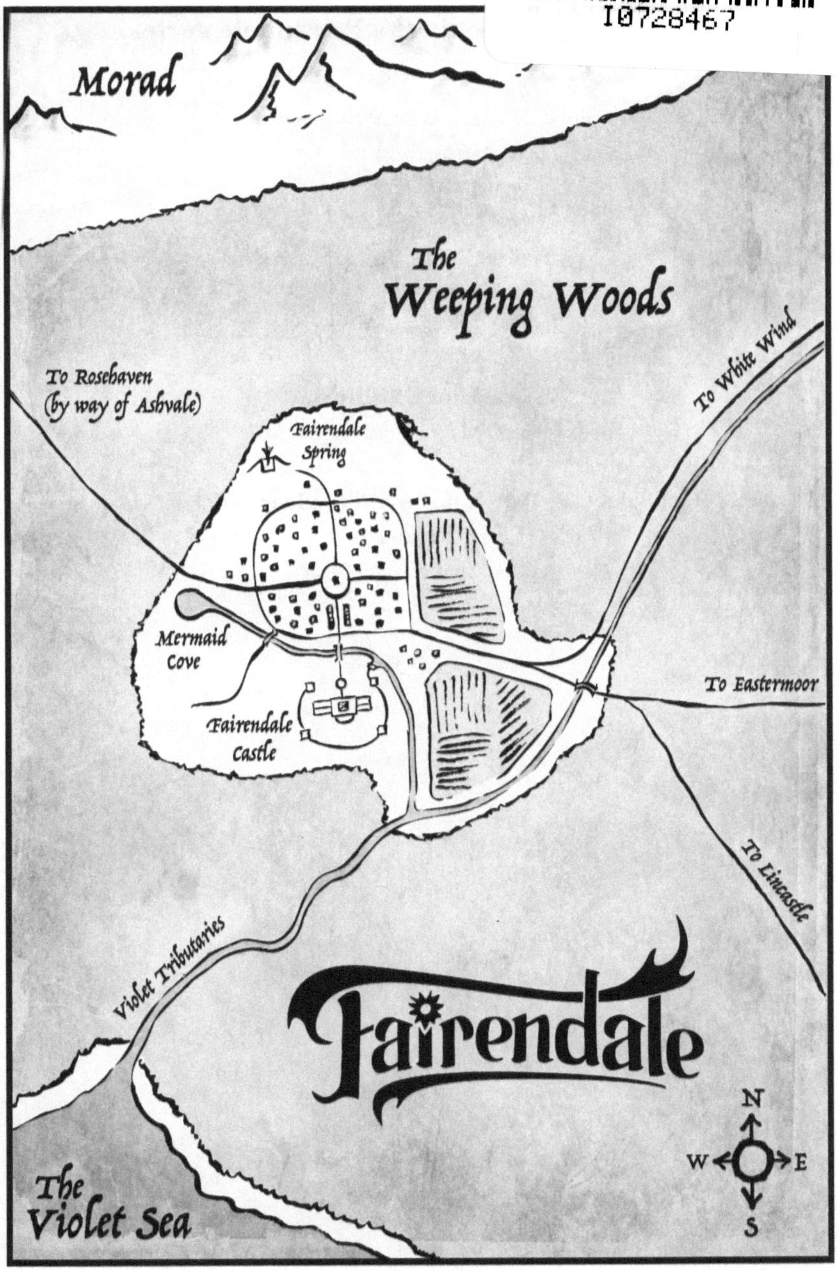

Morad
The Weeping Woods
To Rosehaven
(by way of Ashvale)
To White Wind
Fairendale Spring
Mermaid Cove
Fairendale Castle
To Eastermoor
To Lincastle
Violet Tributaries
Fairendale
The Violet Sea
N
W E
S

Read all the books in the Fairendale series!

Book .5: *The Good King's Fall (a prequel)*
Book 1: *The Treacherous Secret*
Book 2: *The King's Pursuit*
Book 3: *The Perilous Crossing*
Book 4: *The Dragons of Morad*
Book 5: *The Fiery Aftermath*
Book 6: *The Mysterious Separation*

Collector's Editions:
Books 1-6: *The Flight of the Magical Children*

To see all the books L.R. Patton has written, please click or visit the link below:
www.lrpatton.com/store

Fairendale

4

THE DRAGONS OF MORAD

Batlee Press
PO Box 591596
San Antonio, TX 78259

Printed in the United States of America

First Edition—2016/Cover designed by Toalson Marketing
www.toalsonmarketing.com

L.R. PATTON

THE DRAGONS OF MORAD

BATLEE PRESS

*To my dragons,
who set a world
afire*

Footsteps

They say dragons can feel footsteps. It matters not how silent those footsteps may be, for it is said that dragons can feel the shifting of the earth, even if it is but a gentle shifting. The children, and, of course, Arthur and Maude, know very well these stories, and so it is that they travel on the perimeter of Morad with a mounting fear in their hearts. Will they wake the dragons? Will they find themselves in a greater danger than they might ever have faced? Will they have the utmost privilege of bearing witness to the majesty of creatures such as these, a privilege that comes with a dangerous price?

The answers to these questions do not matter at all, dear reader, for Arthur and Maude and the children know they must journey on. They know that passing through the dragon lands of Morad is the only way. They know that the king's guard, under orders from King Willis to find the magical boy of

Fairendale, are coming for them, and to turn back would be to surrender their lives. They must move forward. They must at least try.

Arthur leads the way. He steps carefully, slowly, silently. No one speaks a single word. They are afraid of speaking, you see, for any noise could be the noise that gives them away. If they could fly through this land, they would, for even the noise of their feet, the shaking of those steps, carries danger. They cannot very well keep the ground from shifting beneath them. Who could?

There are so many children, and they are trying so very hard to be quiet, but children, we well know, are not always skilled at keeping quiet, nor are they always skilled at knowing precisely what quiet means. One has only to recall the experience of slipping out of bed, for one more thing, and immediately being discovered by one's parents to agree that this is an interesting mystery, indeed.

A dragon's ear, alas, is even finer tuned than a parent's.

Arthur leads the children onward toward a shelter. He has chosen a cave. There are many in this land, but this cave is larger than all the others, enough to hold the twenty-four children and the two grown ones. He does not speak his fear aloud, not only because he knows the gift of silence in a land such as this one, but also because he does not want to alarm the children. There could be dragons waiting in that cave. Oh, yes. But perhaps fortune will smile upon them today, as it seems to have smiled upon them in their every attempt to escape danger. This is the hope Arthur carries. Every step, this hope trades places with his fear, so his footsteps sound like this:

Left, right, left, right, left, right. Fear, hope, fear, hope, fear, hope.

Maude brings up the tail end. The children stretch between them. They do not run, hardly even walk, to be precise. They creep, one step after another. The girls do not touch their staffs to the ground, for that would be unnecessary noise. They cradle them in their arms instead. The children think only of what is behind them, hoping that they have gained enough space between them and the danger of the king's men that they will not be discovered. It is not so very far to the cave before them, but they move so slowly.

Maude, for her part, thinks only of the dragons. Perhaps Arthur, Maude and the children will be permitted this invasion. Perhaps the dragons are reasonable creatures who will listen to their story and agree that they may pass into lands of safety. She looks around the wasteland that has not moved or changed at all in the minutes they have traveled. Not a single sign of life. And this brings another concern to the mind of a woman like Maude. What is it that they will eat? Where will they find water?

How will they survive this crossing without sustenance?

And what will they do once they reach the cave? They will not be able to remain in a cave forever. What is it Arthur has planned? Has he planned at all?

She supposes her husband has likely not thought this through in its entirety, but she cannot blame him, reader. For they are all only concerned with the moment, with ensuring safety here and now. They will consider the future when they have reached safety.

And look. They have made it to the mouth of the cave. Maude has caught up to the group, and they are standing in a huddle of sorts. Arthur glances behind them, to make sure no one has followed them. In fact, he looks all around, briefly, with a trained eye that has not been used for some time. It has been many years since he has seen a dragon. He has forgotten how to look.

"I shall go in first," Arthur whispers, and Maude nods silently. Brave Arthur. He is a good man, a kind man, and, perhaps most importantly, a courageous man. Not many would risk their lives for all these children. But Arthur has risked his life all along the way and now risks his life by walking into a cave.

Caves, you see, are the homes of dragons. He remembers this from his days as a boy, when he would move about in caves, always stepping silently and carefully to ensure there was no danger inside. Sometimes, as a young boy, he found that danger in sleeping form, and he found himself fleeing without a backward glance.

It takes him only a moment, and then Arthur is beckoning them all to enter. "Quickly," he says. "Let us seek cover."

It is dark inside the cave. If one could see inside it, one might note how very like the dungeons beneath the dungeons this cave appears. It is dark and cold and damp. These children, who have escaped from the king's men, face the same sort of sleeping place as the children who did not escape. This, dear reader, is what one might call irony.

One of the girls, a quiet one called Minnie, musters enough magic, though she is tired and starving, to make the tip of her staff glow. The children look around them, but do not see much before Maude, dear Maude, closes a fist over the girl's staff. "No," she says. "We must not use light. We cannot risk being discovered."

Will the children have to live in the dark forever? This is the fear that creeps into all of their hearts. They squint their eyes, but there is nothing to see, for the light lessens the deeper they move into the cave, the further they creep from the mouth. A cave as long as this quickly loses all its light.

"This cave is larger than it first appeared," Arthur says. The children only know where he is by the sound of his voice. They run their hands against the sides of the cave, feeling their way forward. It grows narrower the deeper they move. "There will be plenty of space for all of us to sleep."

The children brush up against one another, but they cannot see whose tunic touches whose dress or whose foot steps on theirs or which arm has hooked their elbow, for it is much too dark. They cannot even see the whites of their eyes anymore. It is as if the light has been drained from their world.

"Sit, children," Arthur says. "You are tired. We must rest for a time."

In truth, all the children want is a bit of water. If you will remember, they have only just finished running faster than they have, perhaps, ever run in their lives, and their mouths are dry and parched. Arthur seems to sense this, or perhaps he feels the same, for he says, "I will search for some water." A clinking noise. A step. A whisper.

"It is far too dangerous," Maude says, and it is so quiet in the cave that all the children hear her.

"It is dangerous to live without water as well," Arthur whispers. "I must go."

And then he is gone, and it is Maude bidding the children to lie down and rest.

And they try, dear reader. They certainly do. But, you see, this ground is not the same as their underground home. Their underground home had beds made of straw, at least. Here, the only bed they find is one of rock. The edges prod their backs. For a time, there is only the sound of children trying to find a comfortable position, but soon, they stop trying, for there is no comfortable position when one is lying on cold, hard, knobby rock.

"It is not like our other home," Hazel whispers into the dark. The children murmur around her.

Her mother finds her hand and squeezes it, though Hazel can only sense that the hand in hers is her mother's, for she cannot see it. "We will leave for Rosehaven soon," Maude says. "We have only to stay here until we are sure the way is safe. The king's men will move on."

"What about food?" a boy calls from the darkness. "What shall we do for food?"

"Arthur will see to that," Maude says. "Do not worry about your well being. He has brought us here because he knows this land."

The children, more than anyone, know the stories of Arthur's wanderings, for this is how they passed their time underground, with storytelling. Arthur is the greatest of all storytellers, though not one of them can recall hearing any involving dragons or these lands.

"Has he traveled across Morad?" Hazel says.

"Many, many years ago," Maude says.

"Did he know the dragons?" a girl asks.

"He did not know them," Maude says. "But they let him pass."

This gives the children great hopes for their own safe passage, as one might imagine. If Arthur crossed these lands once, and the dragons did not stop him, perhaps they, who are in grave danger, will be permitted to cross. It is this very hope, in fact, that led Arthur to try these lands, for no man would ever think to look here.

"How will we cross the land?" a boy says.

Though Maude would like nothing more than for the children to sleep, for she has worries of her own, she knows that they are frightened, and a child frightened is a child who cannot sleep. So she says, "From cave to cave. We will run on silent feet and hide in the darkness."

"I do not like the dark," a girl calls out in a squeaky voice.

"No," Maude says. "Not many do. But darkness is our safety now, children. At least until we cross these lands."

Someone's stomach rumbles. A few of the children laugh. Others weep. They are so very hungry, you see. So thirsty. So afraid.

Hazel is glad her mother's hand rests on hers. She pulls her head against her mother's shoulder now. "I do not want to leave

Fairendale," she says. "It is all I have ever known."

Her mother strokes her hair. "I know, my dear," Maude says. "But you were born in Rosehaven. You do not remember, but you loved the land once."

"Is it as lovely as Fairendale?" Hazel says.

"No," Maude says. "I have never seen a land as lovely as Fairendale, though I have not seen them all. And Fairendale…" She does not finish, but every child here could finish for her. Fairendale is not as lovely as it once was. They have heard the stories from their own parents, you see. Fairendale, as it existed once, practically shimmered with vibrant colors and clear skies. And while it is true that the Fairendale before the king's roundup wore vibrant colors and beautiful blue skies, it did not shimmer as it had done once upon a time. The land had never known a cloud until King Sebastien took the throne. Some stories say it was his doing, that he did not enjoy the light so much as The Good King Brendon, and that is why clouds crept in. The children have never known this flawless world. They have only known a muted beauty that is, still, lovelier than all other lands.

Fairendale has grown even darker still, now, without the children, but they have not gone back to see it. They do not know what a land becomes without its children.

"But the people of Rosehaven are good people," Maude says. "They will keep us safe. They will grant us asylum."

Hazel does not speak again. She is only thinking of Theo. What if they never find Theo? What if he does not know where they have gone? What if he is in the king's possession?

What if he dies?

She cannot bear to think of her brother's death. She cannot bear to think of life without him, of magic without him. She does not dare say her thoughts aloud, for she does not want to cause her mother more distress. So she says, instead, "What if we do not ever return to Fairendale?"

"I believe we shall," Maude says. "In time. In the days of another king, perhaps."

"A king like Prince Virgil?" Hazel says.

"Perhaps another," Maude says. Her voice has grown far away, as if she is no longer in the cave but with her husband, who, even now, is stealing back to their cave on legs that belong to a much younger man.

"You must rest, my dear," Maude says. "I shall wait up for your father. I will guard the way." She gently pushes her daughter away from her shoulder. Hazel stretches out on the ground, as all the children have done, their feet touching heads, on and on down the line, each of them facing another, but for the last one, a boy called Jasper, whose head points toward the mouth of the cave, though still deep enough inside to be hidden from those who might peer in from the outside.

Soon, the cave will grow much darker, for the sun will be gone, but the children will not notice, for they are very tired— tired enough, even, to sleep on a bed of stone. They do not think of the dark, nor of the stone, nor of what may come tomorrow. They merely sleep, their breaths warming the cave.

No one but Maude hears Arthur return. No one but Maude hears Arthur whisper. "It is growing colder out there. And we are headed north. But I brought us water." No one but Arthur hears Maude whisper back.

"We will make it, will we not, Arthur? We will make it to Rosehaven. Please tell me we will."

Only Arthur and Maude hear the silence that stretches between them, summoned by a question that cannot be answered.

In the woods, hidden quite impressively, away from any place one might detect him even if one were skilled in looking, is a man.

He is a young man, clothed in brown and green and all the colors of the forest that turn him invisible to the naked eye. He has donned his cover most skillfully, huddling in the shadows, right out in the open, but one would never notice anything but a stump.

This man is an unknown man. He does not dare move from his cover. He must appear as a stump, if he is to watch the mouth of the cave unnoticed. He must not retreat back into the trees. He must certainly not step over the line. He knows the rules, after all. He knows that no man who desires to live would ever cross this boundary line.

And so he hides. And waits.

He waits for what he knows must come.

For he has seen the print. His kind can see prints from quite a distance away.

It is only a matter of time.

In the heart of the woods, the king's men have dared remain longer inside the cover of trees than any other man, for they have been given a charge, and they, in truth, feel desperate to find the missing children, for the ones among them who have lives in the village of Fairendale, which is merely a handful of them, want nothing more than to return to their wives and mothers. They are duty bound, and these men, you see, are honorable men, unwilling to break their vows to their king, though their king has stolen some of their children. It is not easy to understand, is it, dear reader? But honor is a strange thing, different for every man. Some believe that honor means fulfilling the duty they have promised another. Some believe that honor means caring for their families. These men, you see, are caught between the two. Fulfilling a duty is what they are doing. Caring for their families is also what they are doing. One might argue that the king's men are not caring for their families, but in the world of Fairendale, one who works for the king is one who receives all his family needs. Alas, they cannot decide between finding their own children and caring for the family that is left to them. And so they do their duty. They hold to their honor.

They look rather silly cavorting about in their silver breastplates and clunky armor, trying to beat the sun. The men who are strictly soldiers and the men who are also family men have all heard the stories of the dangers that live in these woods, and so they turn stones and climb trees and crawl on their hands and knees, noses near the ground in full soldier dress, for protection, of course (they did not dare take it off, for what if they should meet a creature of the wood?). They search in a fashion that is decidedly hurried and desperate, for they must find their way out before the sun disappears. And the light is fast fading, for the trees loom thick and tall.

The children, it seems, have vanished into thin air. There is not a trace of them, thanks to magic.

Sir Greyson and his men are tired. They have been looking for so long, day after day after day, with nothing new to report to a king who grows angrier by the hour. King Willis, as we know by now, is not a patient man, and he cannot understand why the children have not yet been found, why the king's men lost them in the first place, though if you remember, the king's men lost the children because of the disappearance of the king's own son and a call that divided the soldiers in half.

Every day the children remain missing is another day the children travel farther into the arms of safety, but, to the king's men, it is another day the guard travels farther from those arms, for the king could very well decide to rid himself of all these men who have failed him. Captain Sir Greyson knows how uncertain his future is. He knows how uncertain his mother's future is. This is why he continues searching for the missing children, for he does not, truth be told, want to find the children at all. If not for his mother, who suffers from the sugar sickness and is only alive because of the medicine Sir Greyson receives from the castle, he would abandon this search entirely.

Perhaps, if the king could tell Sir Greyson what it is he intends to do with the children, Sir Greyson might change his mind. Or perhaps not. Sir Greyson has always loved children, though he never had any of his own. He has never seen the dungeons beneath the dungeons. He can only imagine how dark and damp and unforgivable a place such as that one can be. He has asked the boy, Calvin, who takes food and water to the children, what it is the boy finds on his descents into these dungeons. Calvin has reported that the children grow more frightened by the day, for no child wants to live forever in a place where they cannot see the very finger that scratches their nose. Sir Greyson knows that the king will not allow captured children to live in comfort until the one with magic is found. And even then, it is not a guarantee that the others will be released.

And so it is that our good captain of the king's guard does not perform his duties as well as he might, in another circumstance, perform them. He has seen the looks of the villagers. He has seen the way Fairendale has changed since the children disappeared. He has seen the look in his king's eye, desperate to keep a throne at all costs.

There is mourning and there is darkness and there is greed all around.

Sir Greyson knows what side he wants to be on, what side he would be on, if not for the letter. This morning it arrived from the village healer. His mother would not last much longer, it said. Not without stronger medicine. Not without a return of the light. And the light will not return without the children. He does not know this for certain, but a man can sense these kinds of things.

Tell me, dear reader, what is it you would do? Leave the children to their escape, ensuring your mother's death, or find them, hoping that you will be able to save them yet?

So it is that Sir Greyson continues his duty. So it is that he orders his men to continue looking under every stone and tree and crack of the earth. So it is that they search for a piece, just a tiny trace of the missing children to lend all the king's men hope and relief.

Meanwhile, the day passes on and night hastens toward them.

Sir Greyson looks around at his men. There is his second in command, Sir Merrick, a good man with a daughter who disappeared. There is his rear guard, a man who lost three children in the roundup. There is the man whose wife has not risen from her bed since the day his baby girl was taken. He can see how defeated they are. He can sense how very near they have come to giving up. He has noticed their surreptitious glances toward the village, where everything they love waits for men who may or may not return at the end of day.

"Sir," says Sir Merrick.

Sir Greyson turns to him. "Yes, Sir Merrick?" he says. Sir Merrick points toward the sky. Sir Greyson had not noticed, before now, how dark it had become.

"We must move from these woods soon," Sir Merrick says.

Yes. They must. He nods at Sir Merrick, who lets out a long whistle. The men turn to face Sir Greyson and Sir Merrick, their armor clanking and ringing with a noise that echoes through the woods and makes the silence within the trees seem ever more dangerous.

Sir Greyson lets out a long breath. The king would not be pleased that they had found nothing this day, but he cannot risk keeping his men in the forest after sundown. He lifts his voice loud enough to be heard by the men at the outer edges. "Hear me, men!" he says. They stand silently, looking toward their captain. They trust Sir Greyson completely, these men, for he is a good man. A good man is a good leader. "We must return to the castle. The sun will not light the way much longer." The men involuntarily shiver, a sound that spreads through the wood like a clanging of muted bells. The men know that dusk is the most magical time of all, when eyes could play tricks on minds and one could not know whether what one was seeing was real or imagined until it was too late. The woods had been known to keep grown men, not just children. They have heard about the horrors that crawl from their daytime hiding places. They know about the imps and trolls and creatures that cannot be named, for no name even exists to describe them.

The men begin to mount their horses, sending up a great roar of armor lifting up and out and catching at the top of the boughs as if no sound is permitted to leave the cover of trees. They ready their horses for running, which they will, now, have to do in order to beat the dusk.

And in the middle of all the noise comes a small voice, almost too small to be heard, snaking into Sir Greyson's ear.

"Here," it says.

"What was that?" Sir Greyson says to his men. They, too, stop to listen. "Did someone speak?"

The men look around, not one of them claiming the voice Sir Greyson heard.

"Here," the voice says again. "Footprints."

Sir Greyson turns toward the place from where the voice seems to come. But there is nothing. No one.

And then Sir Merrick says, "There."

He points. Sir Greyson follows his arm. Off to the side, emerging from a cloud of sorts, though it is, perhaps, only fog gathering in the light of dusk, is a small, bent old woman.

A old sorceress, perhaps. Sir Greyson has never seen one quite so old. But her face, its lines and its nose and its gleaming, hungry eyes, remind him of pictures he has seen in story books.

"Leave us, old woman," Sir Greyson says. "We must be on our way."

"But they are here," the old woman says. Her eyes, the bluest eyes he has ever seen, reach into his and pull, pull, pull, until he cannot look away. Sir Greyson can feel the eyes of his men trained on him, can feel the eyes of the woman drawing him closer. She is ugly and old and bent in two, undesirable in every way but for those blue eyes that remind him so much of his queen's.

It is not Queen Clarion. She is much too old, much too bent. It is an illusion. Sir Greyson tries to turn away, but her spell, if that is what she has stretched around him, will not permit him such an easy escape.

"The children are here," the old woman says.

"Where?" Sir Merrick calls out. He, it seems, has not been bewitched at all. His wits are still about him. "Where are they?"

Behind him, Sir Greyson can feel his men breathing hard. They are anxious to leave these woods. They are anxious to keep their lives, truth be told, and the forest does not promise their lives at all.

Sir Greyson cannot turn, cannot order them to leave, cannot move at all. He is held by a blinding blue.

Sir Merrick climbs from his horse, places his hand on his captain's shoulder. "Where, woman?" Sir Merrick says.

She points to the ground, her eyes leaving Sir Greyson's for a moment. He backs away. "Here," she says.

Sir Merrick bends over the spot where the woman has pointed. Yes. There it is. A footprint. How is it that they missed this? How is it that they could not see this flattened grass, this raised dirt, this proof that someone has walked here? Sir Greyson looks, too, and suddenly he sees them all, so many footprints, so many marks, so many children, running all in the same direction.

The children. They have found the children.

The old woman cackles. Sir Greyson's armor clatters as he startles, so lost was he in thought. Have they really found the children? Have they really found a way? How is it that they can leave now? He looks at his men, up at the sky, back toward the prints.

"The footprints of children and those who wish to protect them," the old woman says, "can only be seen by the light of the moon."

She points to the sky. Sir Greyson and all his men look up. Yes, the moon has uncovered its light. It reaches fingers down, into the woods, illuminating all the prints. The forest has grown suddenly and unexpectedly dark. A wolf howls. The trees come rustling alive, and by alive, it might surprise you that I mean they open their eyes. A fog grows behind all the king's men, obscuring their way forward.

Sir Greyson does the only thing he can think to do. He flings his sword into the ground, the hilt pointed in the direction the footprints lead, and then swings a foot over his saddle and sits heavily down.

He and his men race from the forest to the music of an old woman cackling, a wolf howling, and unknown terrors beating in pursuit.

Fortune

Cora was not like the other girls. In fact, the other girls stayed away from the likes of her, for she was unusual with her flame-red hair and her glowing green eyes, and they all said she was a magician who was not like the other magicians but was, instead, dangerous—one to be avoided.

Well, she did have magic. And no one really knew it for sure, but she knew she *was* skilled enough at her magic to practice the dark arts as well, though they held danger.

She had the most powerful magic in the land of Fairendale, at least before the little girl Clarion came to live in the kingdom. Cora could shape shift, which no one could do, for there were rules to magic. If one conjured a vanishing spell or attempted shape-shifting without the natural gift, one could not know if they would ever walk in their original shape again. The first time she tried shape shifting, after a strange and foreign prophetess whispered the possibility in her ear, she had been terrified. The first time she flew she did not know if she would ever touch the ground again.

But she did.

And soon it became quite easy for her to slip in and out of her skin. One moment she wore the milky robes of the beautiful girl she was becoming and the next she wore the black feathers of a bird. She could not let people see her do it, however, for they did not trust the kind of magic that could shift shapes. So she tempered what she could do and never whispered to a soul. That meant she did not have many friends, and a girl without friends is a girl mostly without hope.

She slipped in and out of her skin every night, and she would fly about the forest and the dragon lands, memorizing sights she could not look upon by day. She considered crossing to other lands, but she knew that in some places people hunted birds like her, for they found them bad omens, and so she stayed well within the bounds of Fairendale, which had no fear of blackbirds, at least not then. She was in the sky the night she saw a mermaid for the first time. Good fortune. That is what the mermaids meant. Good fortune to those who saw them in the darkness, or those who caught their tail at the evening's last light. She saw them every night, pointing to the sky, pointing to her, in fact. Mermaids were said to know things no humans could know, so, perhaps they had guessed her secret. No matter. Mermaids were not known for telling secrets.

Though she was a lonely child, Cora had her father, who loved her dearly. And for a while, that was enough.

One night, when Cora was only a babe, the king's men came to her father's cottage and told him that the king requested his services at the castle. Her father had been a cook once upon a time, though he was far too old now. He did not argue, of course, but Cora knew he had hoped his cooking would be done by now.

That was the first night the king's men had visited her father. But there was another.

During this second visit, Cora was in bed when they came. Her father left with the men that night, for the king had requested audience with him. The parents of Fairendale, you see, did not think twice about leaving their young children alone. Children were always safe. There were always watchful eyes trained on them. They would not be taken or harmed by anyone, for the people trusted one another. What is a community without trust?

But Cora did not remain that night in her bed. She stole out, for she heard the voices. She followed her father in her feathery form, and watched the entire interview, her father in King Sebastien's throne room, from a window. And King Sebastien had the kind of voice that could carry right through a pane of glass, so Cora did not have trouble hearing what was said.

"Your daughter has powerful magic," the king was saying.

Her father dipped his head. "Yes," he said.

"We would like to propose a union," the king said.

Even in her bird heart, Cora felt the excitement. She had always wanted to rule a kingdom, you see. She had always wanted to save Fairendale from the hands of a man like King Sebastien. She knew one of his sons to be good and kind. The other, she did not know. So she hoped the union would be made with the one who would rule.

"A union?" her father said. His eyes changed. She peered through the window. They were wary. Unsure.

"To my son Willis," the king said, and Prince Willis bowed to her father. He was not an ugly boy, though his brother was much more handsome. She could not recall if this one was the first son or the second. Had they been twins?

It did not matter so much. She would still be a princess. She could use her strong will to persuade her future husband, this future king, to rule in kindness once the evil King Sebastien was out of the way. She would prosper. She had seen the mermaids' tail, after all.

Good fortune had finally come to pass. So she flew back home to wait for her father.

When her father returned, he was surprised to see his daughter still awake. "Cora," he said. "You should be in bed."

"Father," she said. "Tell me your news of the castle."

"How did you know I was summoned to the castle?" her father said. He looked at her with all sorts of questions in his eyes, but Cora merely shook her head. "I heard them come."

Her father's eyes crinkled a bit, into the smile she loved so. And then they grew serious. "The king," he said, "wants to pledge you in marriage to his son."

"The second or the first?" Cora said.

Her father looked confused. "Are they not twins?" he said. "I thought them to be." He looked past Cora, as if he could no longer see his daughter.

"It matters not," Cora said. "Only what did you say?"

Her father took her hand. "I said that I would talk to my daughter."

Cora smiled. Her father. What a kind man he was. She kissed his cheek. "Yes, father," she said. "Yes, I will become a princess."

Her father leaned forward, tipping her chin up so her eyes were level with his. "He is not the handsome one," he said. "Nor is he the particularly kind one."

She shook her head. "I care not, Father," she said. "You have taught me well. I can always be kind. I can teach him to be kind as well."

Her father leaned back in his chair. "Yes, well," he said. "I am afraid it is not so easy as that."

She patted her father's knee. "Please tell the king yes, Father," Cora said. "I would make this kingdom beautiful and happy as it once was."

Her father looked at her with all the love he held in his heart. "Yes," he said. "Yes, I believe you might."

And that is how Cora became engaged to Prince Willis.

Fortune, it seems, was finally on her side.

She could not have been more wrong.

Throne

Back at the castle, King Willis has been stricken with a generous streak. Do you see him, reader, standing on his platform, letting his son sit the throne? Do you see him step back, tilt his head and study his son? Do you see the way Prince Virgil clutches the arm rests as if he will never let go?

Can you see his smile? For it is the brightest light in the room. What the children in the dungeon and the children trying to sleep in a cave would give for a light such as this one.

King Willis, you see, knows the power that lives in his throne.

It is a strange power. A knowing power. A desired power, one that latches onto the most pliable of hearts and burrows in deep. Some men, you see, can master its power. But some men are mastered by its power.

Which is it Prince Virgil will be? It is hard to tell just yet.

And it is true that this power is not what it used to be, as is the case with so much in the land of Fairendale. The throne, you see, is where a certain King Sebastien used to repose. And because King Sebastien used to repose here, the very fibers of this throne have altered. They became a small bit harsher. Crueler. More inhuman perhaps.

Those who sit on this throne are forever changed, one way or another. The kind become kinder. The brave become braver. The greedier become greedier.

This throne forever wrestles with light and dark, and it is a person's heart that has the final say. But Prince Virgil's heart, you see, is still being shaped, by the hands of Queen Clarion, who has not yet given up, and by the hands of King Willis, who has begun in earnest to leave his mark upon it more so than he has ever done. He has seen that it is time.

So what is it we would see, if we could see the fibers of this throne? Would we see light, or would we see dark?

Well, it is both.

Prince Virgil, you see, is a boy like his mother and like his father. Queen Clarion is a woman of virtue and honor and everything that is good and beautiful, and his father, well. His father was not always this way. He was a good and kind and honorable boy once upon his time, before his brother was banished and a father trained him for the throne.

Believe it or not, the first time King Willis sat this throne, he saw what Prince Virgil sees. A brighter world, dimming only at the corners. And every sit the king permitted him, the corners grew dimmer.

It is what King Willis plans for his own son.

But for now, Prince Virgil sits on the throne, grips the sides, rests his back against its cold gold and stares right into the confines of his heart, though he does not know at what he looks. He sees the light. He sees the dark. He watches them wrestle. Back and forth, over and over, light and dark.

And light, today, wins.

Prince Virgil sits, and he listens to his father go on and on and on about the responsibility of running a kingdom, how there are certain matters that must be tended every day, and people who must be managed every day and decisions that must be made every hour. Prince Virgil's mind wanders, for his father, you see, loves to talk, and he knows that he does not need to listen to every single word to hear what his father says. He will hear him the same, but he will think, too. He thinks that he has not seen many people knocking on the doors of the castle, ever. The only ones who travel to and fro are the king's men. In fact, he cannot recall his father settling any disputes or making any decisions that did not involve food since Prince Virgil was old enough to save memories. How hard must it be to run a kingdom?

King Willis moves on to the food and the sweet rolls and all the grand delicacies that a boy could ever want, and this is where Prince Virgil's mind wanders ever more. For he has seen the children in the village, how some had only a loaf of bread to eat at their noonday meal, while the castle has always had more food than can possibly be eaten in a day's entirety. It seems wasteful to Prince Virgil, to carry on in such a way.

As if he has heard the thoughts of his son, King Willis moves on to what he calls the most important matters of running a kingdom, and that is keeping the people in their proper place.

"A king," he says, "is not a wish giver."

Yes. Prince Virgil has heard these words before. He stretches his legs out before him.

"A king does not simply give people food. They must work for it." King Willis looks on his son with something that could quite possibly be interest, though he has never shown the slightest bit in the recent past. Perhaps he has come to an understanding that his time on the throne is nearing its end. Prince Virgil will be ready to sit the throne in only four years' time.

The prince looks on the windows that line the throne room. It has grown darker outside, near enough to black that the boy grows antsy. He does not want to miss the first star. So he stands from the throne.

His father turns, and now that Prince Virgil has risen from the spell of his father's throne, he can see more clearly. He sees his father, large and growing larger, and he thinks of Arthur and Maude, thin enough to nearly get lost in a doorway. His heart aches with a longing that surprises him. What he would give for one of Maude's cookies.

What he would give to see his friend Theo.

King Willis is smiling. "What did you think, son?" he says. "Was it merely wonderful or…magnificent?"

We know well enough that the king has used words that are not so different from one another at all, dear reader. King Willis, however, does not see the similarities between the two. He was not so good at language lessons, you see.

Prince Virgil does not think it was either, really. It was cold. And hard. And what is the word he seeks? Difficult? Unsettling? Terrifying?

Why, it is all three.

But he would never tell his father, of course, so he says, "Magnificent." He hopes his father will be pleased enough with that.

But his father appears disappointed. Perhaps he has noticed the brightness of Prince Virgil's eyes. Perhaps he has somehow sensed his son's sadness, though he is not a man much given to these kinds of emotions any longer. Once, perhaps. But no longer. The throne, you see, stole more than light from him.

"Well," King Willis says. "Well, then."

"It is time for my supper," Prince Virgil says, though he is not in the least bit hungry. "I must go."

"Stay," King Willis says. "Sup with me."

Oh, reader. Prince Virgil wants nothing more than to please his father, but this, you see, he cannot do, for he has not the stomach this night. Perhaps another time.

"I cannot," Prince Virgil says. "Mother is waiting."

"Your mother can wait," King Willis says.

"Please, father," Prince Virgil says.

"Very well then," King Willis says. As you can see, he is in a very generous mood this eve. "There are many more opportunities to sup with me."

King Willis folds into the throne again, tucking himself around the arm rests as if he were a plush doll to be molded and positioned into all the corners. Prince Virgil looks away until his father is no longer moving, and then he turns back. He would like to leave his father now, truth be told, but he knows that his father has more to say. And he is correct.

"When my father was a boy," King Willis says, "he was very poor." King Willis clears his throat, as if unaccustomed to telling stories such as this one. And, truth be told, he is. "My grandmother died because my father's father was so poor. She would have yet lived if my father had become king sooner."

Prince Virgil wonders, then, why it is that his father would not feel some responsibility for the poor. Why had his grandfather forbidden the feeding of the poor? Why would they both not ensure that the poor were fed and cared for in a way his grandfather's mother had not been?

Our prince, you see, has much to learn about this world in which he was born.

"My father worked very hard for this throne," King Willis says. "He worked for his wealth. He trained men for years. He braved the dangers of the Violet Sea and crossed it." King Willis pauses in this story, for he knows that this is a feat to be admired, though, if one were to travel back in time, one would know that King Sebastien never even set a foot in the Violet Sea. Prince Virgil, though, has already heard these stories from his mother, and the one he hasn't—about his grandfather crossing the Violet Sea—he does not believe. King Willis, disappointed, continues. "He marched through the dragon lands and felled dragons. He did something. He risked his life. He could never abide those who did nothing. He could never abide the poor."

"But some do not have magic as he did," Prince Virgil says. "What could they do?"

"There is always something one can do," King Willis says.

"There is always work to be done. One must be resourceful. Industrious. Smart."

"Like Arthur," Prince Virgil says. He claps a hand over his mouth, for he did not mean to say it. The words came out of their own accord. He had never known anyone as resourceful or industrious or smart.

"The woodworker," King Willis says. He tilts his head, examining his son. "You think him a good example of the kingdom?" There is a tinge of anger in the king's voice. Prince Virgil shakes his head.

"I did not mean—" he says.

"I could tell you otherwise," King Willis says. "But I will let time do its work." The king is silent for a moment, until he says, in a softer, lower, and somehow more frightening voice: "He stole the children. He escaped with them. He is only a traitor. As every poor man eventually shows himself to be."

Prince Virgil does not say anything, though he is burning to ask questions.

What if poor people have nothing with which to be resourceful?

What is it his father hates so much about the poor?

What does he know of them at all?

He would begin with all of those. But he drops his head and studies the ground.

"You know nothing of the poor," King Willis says then. "You know nothing of ruling a throne. But you will learn." Prince Virgil raises his eyes. His father is looking on him with eyes that are very nearly black. "You will learn."

Yes, he will learn. But what is it, exactly, that he will learn? Is it mercy? Is it hate? Is it something sinister and cold? Is it something gentle and warm?

Time will do its work, and we are powerless to stop it.

Prince Virgil, in truth, does not know if he has what it might take to sit the throne of Fairendale, for he considers himself kind, for the most part, though he was not so very kind on the last meeting he had with his friends. He would change that if he could. Oh, yes, he would. And for this, we can momentarily feel glad.

Prince Virgil dips his head again. He is done, for now, with this throne room and his father. "May I be excused, Father?" Prince Virgil says. "I must get to Mother."

King Willis looks at him, long and hard. "Enjoy a sweet roll before you go," he says. He waves his hand at Garth, who comes running with a plate, already heaped with the sweet rolls that seem to be in great abundance in the castle, perhaps because of the king's love for them.

Prince Virgil does not argue but takes one of the sweet rolls, though just now he would prefer rye bread hot from the oven with a slab of butter smothered on it, just the way Cook makes his snack in the afternoons. He will miss that snack today, because of this meeting with his father. He eats the roll as quickly as he can, hoping that his father cannot see how tired he he has grown of sweet rolls, and then his father dismisses him.

"Tomorrow," the king calls as his son nears the end of the red carpet. Prince Virgil turns around. His father is still on the throne, eating his third or fourth, or possibly his tenth, roll. "Tomorrow you will come sit the throne again." King Willis knows the power of this throne, the way it will crawl inside his son and dampen the glow of his light. He knows that he will sway his son to his side, if he only has time.

Prince Virgil wishes he could decline this invitation, but it is the king, and, even more, it is his father, and so he dips his head and turns away. He will come late. He will come late in the evening on the morrow, and perhaps the king will forget what he has asked his son to do.

But the king, dear reader, never forgets a thing.

The children wake to whispering. It is not yet fully night. Maude has been unable to sleep, for she has too many worries. Arthur, you see, returned with a bit of water, but he could not gather food, for he could find none. The children cannot survive on only water, and they are too weak to turn the stones to bread.

So Maude whispers. She is not loud, but she is urgent, and children, as children often do, sense her urgency. They sense her fear. They sense that something has gone wrong. Is it Arthur? Is he in danger? They have not seen him since falling asleep, and even still, they cannot see him now.

Hazel turns toward the sound of the whispers. She is the only one close enough to touch her mother, to feel her softness, though all the children can hear the words that are whispered now. The children do not move even the slightest bit, for they do not want to disturb the two. They lie still and listen. And what they hear trails cold fingers down their backs.

"We did not hide our tracks well," Maude says. "The moon will show them."

"No man would dare remain in the woods after dark," Arthur says. "It is too dangerous."

"Perhaps," Maude says. "But King Willis is a desperate man. And desperation can…" She does not say what desperation can do. She merely sighs, and the children are left to draw their own conclusions.

What sort of conclusion might we draw, dear reader? Let us think, for only a moment, what it is that Maude might be saying. Perhaps she would say that desperation can turn a coward brave.

Perhaps she would say that desperation can overcome reason. Perhaps she would say that desperation can make a man, in fact, stay in a dangerous forest far longer than he might otherwise.

"They will not make it out of the forest alive," Arthur says. "And if they did, they would not dare cross the boundary line."

"No one knows if the dragons still exist," Maude says. "We have seen none."

"We do not know if we have seen them," Arthur says. "Dragons are quite skilled at hiding."

"We must run at first light," Maude says. "We cannot keep the children here."

"We must take precautions. We must move slowly," Arthur says. If one could see into the dark, one might see him squeezing the hand of his wife. "Please. Get some sleep. We will talk in the morning. When the children are not sleeping."

"I cannot sleep, Arthur," Maude says. "Not like this." Her whispers have grown louder, more insistent, more terrified, and this, of course, terrifies the children. By now both Arthur and Maude know that she has probably woken them all, though it is not waking time yet, but poor, frightened Maude cannot stop the tide of words from continuing, for there is something she must say, something she must admit, something that has chased her since they first vanished into the forest. "I am afraid."

Oh, dear reader, how wonderful it feels to admit to fear, to disappointment, to anger, to the host of emotions that overtake a human heart. How beautiful it is to unburden oneself, to cease carrying the truth on one's own.

Arthur sits up. He senses that the children are awake. "We must sleep," he says, louder now. "We are safe here. And we need our rest if we are to move on. We must, of course, move on."

Maude, though, cannot rest until she has unburdened it all. "I am more afraid of what the king's men will do when they find us than I am of the dragons," she says. "But I am afraid of the dragons, too." And her words feel like the words of every child in the dark cave, for it is exactly what they feel, too.

"We will tread carefully," Arthur says. "The king's men will not find us. The dragons will not discover we are here. We will escape. If we need it, we have magic."

Yes. They have magic, though it is significantly weakened now. Magic, you see, needs health, and children who starve are not children with health. But the children do not consider this. They merely let the words of Arthur warm their hearts with courage. The girls place a hand on their staffs. The boys close their eyes, knowing that magic is the force that will protect them to the end.

"How is it that we will reach safety?" Maude says. "We merely move from one danger into another."

The children wait. Danger is something they do not quite understand. What is a dragon to them? They are beings from the storybooks, that is all. And what is the king? He is another man, like Arthur, though not like Arthur at all. They do not know the dangers that wait in the hearts of men and the fire of dragons.

"We will move slowly," Arthur says. "With great care. And we will be together."

"We must find another way," Maude says. "Around this land, around the forest."

"There is no other way," Arthur says. "We have gone the only way forward. It is the safest place we can be."

The children ponder this. Are they, in fact, safer in the forbidden lands of Morad than they were in the Weeping Woods?

Well, that is a question our children cannot answer, dear reader. It is a question only time can know.

"One danger into another," Maude says again.

"Such is life," Arthur says. He squeezes his wife's hand and stretches out upon the stone once more. "Children. I brought water. Drink only a bit, and when you are finished, pass this jug back to me."

For a few moments, the only sound is a jug thumping into new hands and children slurping a taste of water. The jug returns to Arthur.

"Lie down now, children," he says. "Sleep. We will think more clearly on the morrow. We will make our plans."

The children do as they are told, though it is not so easy this time to find sleep. Many of them stare into the dark long after others have fallen asleep.

Arthur, too, stares into the dark. And no one can see it, for the cave is much too dark, but Arthur is smiling.

Arthur, you see, has a secret.

Hate

Cora's father worked for King Sebastien, in the kitchens. It was a menial job, to be sure, but it gave them quite enough to eat at night, as her father would bring home batches of what he had cooked in the kitchens. He would even share with the neighbors when he was able to take more than he and Cora needed, which was not often. The king was a stingy man with opinions on whether the villagers needed rich food for free. He did not relish giving his servants more than he thought should be their share.

Sometimes Cora's father would give his own portion to the old widow in the house across from them. Cora would watch him with sadness, and then she would leave a bit of food in her bowl so that he could have something to eat, too. She watched him grow thinner and thinner, and she grew to hate the king more and more every day. Her father would die of starvation before he let his daughter starve. And there he was, in the castle kitchen, surrounded by food every day that he could not eat. It was unjust. Cruel. Maddening.

What kind of king does not care for his people?

One day, when she was a girl of seven, Cora followed her father to the castle. He did not know that she followed, of course, for she braved a daylight shape shifting for once and wore her feathers and trailed him at a safe distance. She watched him walk across the bridge where the mermaids beneath it called out insults about his bones and his skeletal eyes. So already Cora was riled up, for she did not like those who said unkind words to or about her father. She alighted on a window where she knew the kitchens to be. It was open. She watched the door and waited for her father to enter.

When he did, she saw that his eyes were sad. The kitchen was piled high with the best vegetables from the castle gardens and sacks of grain delivered regularly to the castle. He began cutting tomatoes and onions and carrots, probably for some rich stew, for King Sebastien loved soup more than anything else. Her father had told her that his job was fairly simple, for he rotated the same meals every few days. The king was not keen on trying new dishes. So he kept the same ones in an ever-revolving menu. Roast leg of lamb, glazed ham, and stew. That was about all King Sebastien desired.

When her father had finished the chopping and moved on to a hunk of meat that a boy brought in for him, another servant appeared in the doorway.

"The king requires your presence," the man said. He did not use her father's name, Amos. Cora watched her father hunch his shoulders and drop his head. He was so weary. Cora did not like to see her father so weary. He turned to the servant and said, "Yes. Of course. Right away."

And he followed the servant out the door. Cora flew to the other side of the castle, where she knew the throne room to be. This window was open, too, and she perched where those inside could not see her. She waited once more for her father to enter.

When he did, the king clapped his hands. "Cook," he said. He did not use her father's name, either. Did no one call the help by their given names?

"Yes, sire," her father said when he had finally crossed the endless red carpet spread before him and dropped nearly to his knees in a bow.

One day they would be bowing to her like that, even if she were merely a princess. She would show them what power lies in kindness, and the kingdom would love her.

"It is not happy news I bring, alas," the king said. "It is with great sorrow that I tell you we must lock down the possessions of the castle." The king, a handsome man with dark hair and dark eyes and dark skin, leaned forward in his throne. He narrowed his eyes. "We have had reports of stealing."

Her father tilted his head to the side.

"And because there is stealing, we must reduce our risk," King Sebastien said. "So nothing will be carried outside the castle walls."

The king did not seem sorry at all about this news. A smile played across his lips.

Cora watched her father straighten. She could see the muscle in his jaw, turned toward her, twitch. It was the only way she could tell he was angry. Her father was a patient man, mostly agreeable, but he could have a fierce streak now and again. And she could see it coming right at this very moment. "But sire," her father said. "I do not understand."

"The food," the king said. "There will be no more food. A servant has informed us that you take more than your share. That you feed the villagers." The king paused for a moment, as if to let this news, this betrayal, settle in. "The kingdom food is not intended to feed peasants."

Who might have told? Cora knew no one in the castle, but who would betray an old man trying to do the greatest good?

"But sire," her father said. "My daughter."

"Your daughter." The king's face had become a sneer. Perhaps he had forgotten that this man's daughter was promised to the king's son. "Your daughter is nothing."

Cora felt the words dagger her heart, in the places no one could see, and there began a hate so black and so deep and so powerful that she could not rid herself of it. She hated King Sebastien. She hated his son. She hated everything about this castle.

"But—" her father said.

"Silence!" the king roared. "If you value your service here, you will say not another word."

So her father dipped his head once more. And what would he be working for? Enough money to pay for the occasional mending of clothes or shoes that his wife could no longer see to, now that she was dead? What did the king expect of her father? He could not stay at the castle. He could not continue working for a king such as this one.

And yet he did. When the king said, "Do we have an agreement?" her father said, "Yes, sire," and was dismissed. He returned to the kitchen. Cora flew, once more, to the window that opened on it and watched him enter. His eyes streamed with so many tears she had to turn away, for she had only seen her father cry once, the day her mother died.

The hate in her heart grew thicker.

Plans

Cora stands in the center of the village. She is the only one out. The wind blows her flaming red hair, still as red as it always was. It whips around her face, so if one were to look, one would see a girl, rather than a woman approaching middle age.

This woman who appears a girl looks around at all the houses. The flowers have wilted and turned brown. There is not much color left in the village of Fairendale, for the flowers tell a story of joy, and there is no joy to be found in these streets now. The cobblestone path has become riddled with weeds, for there are no feet walking it to temper their growth. The windows are dusty and the doors stand closed. The grass dies. The land is not so beautiful as it used to be.

Fairendale, like the grass, dies. It has been dying since King Sebastien stole the throne, though its dying was much hastened when its children disappeared.

Oh, reader. It truly is tragic.

Cora has heard the talk. The king stole the children because he believed there was a boy of magic born in the village. He searches still, for there were children who escaped. Her daughter, she believes, was one of them. The boy, the rumors say, has yet to be found. So there is hope. A small shred of it, at least.

But, you see, Cora has never been one to wait around for a small shred of hope to do the saving. Cora has always moved, as you may remember. And so move she will again.

She turns from the pitiful sight the land has become, this land she once loved but now cannot bear to look upon, and she moves back into her empty home, where a daughter with hair that flamed as brightly as hers lived once upon a time. It seems so very long ago. Cora misses her daughter, misses the magic that used to be a part of their every day, misses watching her daughter become what she had never been able to become herself, for her daughter was much stronger than Cora had been. Cora never had a teacher like Arthur. He did not come until she was grown, with a magical child of her own. She misses the nighttime ritual she shared with her daughter, when the girl would sit near Cora and ask for stories from the books that line Cora's shelves, for she was always enchanted by stories. Cora runs her hand along their spines and remembers. It is not easy, this remembering.

Is her daughter one of the ones for whom the king searches? Or is she trapped, with the others, in a secret dungeon, as the rumors have suggested of some? There is a boy, you see, who has sent word to his mother about the children, buried beneath the dungeons. No one knows who they are. No one knows who escaped and who did not.

A black cat rubs against Cora's legs. Cora strokes the cat's back. Her daughter never liked old Grimm, but he has been Cora's friend since the days she first practiced magic. He is old and wise and blind. She sits in a chair beside a window, and he settles into her lap.

"We shall find the children, my friend," Cora says. "We shall begin soon." She takes out some parchment, dips a quill into a bottle of ink she has not used in years, and begins her plan. She writes page after page after page, copying the same words and maps and entreaties on all of them. When she is done, she stands and steps through the door of her cottage, careful to grab the last rags of a cape that is fraying badly at the edges, for Fairendale grows colder by the day. Its people are not accustomed to this cold, for the weather has always been predictable, until the sun chose not to rise one day. We know, of course, that the sun always rises, that this is the difference between night and day, but the people of Fairendale are not so sophisticated in their knowledge. They merely know that the sun has vanished, along with their children.

Though she has her cape, though it covers her shoulders in a heavy warmth, Cora shivers through the streets, stooping at the doorway of every home she approaches, sliding the parchment through the generous crack beneath the front doors. She shares her plans with them all, unsure which houses have become empty in these days after the king's thievery. She visits them all, silently speaking her plans, drawing her cape closer about her, though it does no good. It is too cold in these streets. They will need their fires to live soon, and the people have no firewood. They have, in fact, run out of provisions entirely, though they have been tending more diligently than they did before. But the land is dying, you see. They are not producing food so much as they are producing shriveled plants. They are running out of time.

Yes. They are running out of time. And this is what has necessitated Cora's plans. Now she must wait for the people to agree.

When Cora has slipped the parchment beneath every door in the village and is sure none has been forgotten, she moves to the center of the town and then north fifteen paces, uphill, where the great fountains that once gave them an abundance of clear, satisfying water wait for practically nothing, for they have become cloudy and dirty now. The people drink from them, of course, for there is no other water to be found, and one cannot live very long without water. But it is not a satisfying drink, to be sure. And the water runs out, little by little, now only a trickle where once was a rush.

Cora does not look toward the waters. She ducks behind the fountain, crouches to the ground and slips through the magical door made of earth and grass. She waits. She does not know if anyone will come, for her plans are quite aggressive and dangerous.

And at first, the people do not come. Cora waits, alone, in a room that is mostly dark, but for a candle flickering before her. She does not despair, of course, for Cora was never one to despair. Those who act, those who plan, are never bothered by the plans of others, for they know they will do what they plan regardless of how many join them. Such is the determination of Cora.

And then, just before she decides that she must, in fact, execute her plans alone, the earthen walls give a gentle shake. Someone is coming, you see.

The door creaks open. She looks toward it, but she cannot see who enters. She only sees a hood and two eyes peering from beneath it. And then another moves through the door, and another, and another. And suddenly, unexpectedly, the room is full of people, more people than entered it for their last meeting, days ago. More people who are ready, perhaps, to find their children and save the land.

The people lower their hoods, one by one, though it is still cold in this room beneath the ground. Cora recognizes the baker and the shoemaker and the book binder and the town healer, who refused services to the prince, and the gardener and the wives of soldiers who have lived alone all these days. They are all here. They are all here, and she does not realize, until the moment she sees them all and recognizes their faces, how very glad she is that they have come.

She looks at the people crowding this room, and the hope burns as brightly as her hair.

"Welcome," she says.

The people say nothing in return. It is as if the people of Fairendale have forgotten how to speak, if only momentarily. It is as if they have nothing left to say, now that they have seen the plans that could very well demand their lives. They are afraid. They are wretched. But they are also, as one can easily understand, slightly hopeful. For the plans could work. They could save their children, though it may be at the cost of their lives. They will do it, of course. They will do it, because this is what love does.

The room becomes larger in its silence, as if the very walls expand to let them all breathe, to let them all recognize this one moment, where they are joined in a singular purpose.

And then, Bertie, the baker, speaks. "There are more," he says. "I do not think they are coming."

Cora nods her head, just once. She looks around at these brave ones gathered before her. "No matter," she says. "Though we could always use more, we are enough. We will do what must be done and leave the others to their grief." For she knows that the people who have not gathered here have not gathered because of grief, and, perhaps, fear. What else would keep a parent, an adult of any sort, from risking their life to save a child?

"And what is it that must be done?" a woman in the back corner says. Cora cannot see her clearly, but she knows the voice. It is the village rose keeper, who lost three of her children. "We have seen your plans. We are not quite certain what they mean."

Not quite certain what they mean. Cora was sure she had explained her plans clearly.

"We must find the children, of course," Cora says.

"But the king's men have been searching for months," Bertie says. "And they have found nothing." He looks around at the people in the room. He sees, too, their bones jutting through their thin skin. He sees their unbrushed hair, their clothes that hardly fit them, their cloaks that have become rags. The people are dying, too, you see? Even the baker has grown thinner in these days, for it is not easy for him to find wheat. What he does find, what he does bake, he must share with all the people.

"They are not parents," Cora says. A couple of the women draw in sharp breaths. Cora amends her statement quickly. "Rather, not many of them."

"And what does that matter?" says Garron, the gardener. "We do not know where our children are. We do not even know if they live."

"I know," Cora says. "Not a child has died."

"You have the gift?" a woman calls out. "You can See?"

Cora wonders how to answer this question. She was never trained in the gift, you see. But it comes to her now and then. She has Seen the children beneath the dungeons. She has listened to the rumors, and she has watched the picture in her mind, though she cannot be certain it is true at all. Is it not worth pursuing, however? Is it not a worthy cause to explore whether a dungeon beneath the dungeons exists at all?

"No," Cora says. She must tell the truth, after all. "Sometimes I get pictures. I do not know if they lie or tell the truth."

"Then how do we know, either?" Garron says. "How do we find our children?"

"I have seen a dungeon," Cora says. "Not all of them are there, of course. Many of them escaped. But we could free the ones who are caught." She holds up the parchment so they all can see it. "This is how."

"What if we do not succeed?" says a woman with graying hair and dull, brown eyes.

"What if we do not?" Cora says. She looks around at these people she has loved but has never really known, for Cora was never one for knowing people. She breathes. They breathe. The candle flickers between them. "Is it not better to try?"

An old woman, with swollen legs and nearly blue lips, pushes forward. "Yes. It is better to try," she says in a weak and shaking voice. Cora takes her hand, this woman she once loved as a mother herself.

"Come," Cora says. "Please. Lie down." There is a bench in the corner, where the light does not reach. Cora draws the old woman to it, though she knows it will not be comfortable. "You must lie down. You should not be here."

"I must be here," the old woman says. "I must make them see reason." But she lies down and closes her eyes, and she is asleep a moment later.

Cora and the villagers stare across the space between them. Cora does not leave the woman's side, but stands wrapped in shadows. And then Bertie moves forward. "Well, then," he says.

"Let us hear what it is you propose."

Cora moves across the room once more, so as not to disturb the sleeping woman. "Our food is dying," Cora says. "Meanwhile, the king and his royal family feast finely on all the bread they desire and all the soup they need and all the sweet rolls they can fit into their bellies. Our king grows fat while we grow thinner by the hour." She levels her voice, though her heart is full of contempt. She might have married him once upon a time. She might have lived in the castle, been his queen, watched her people starve and been powerless to do anything about it. She does not hold it against Queen Clarion, of course. She knew the queen once. She knows her generous heart.

"Our animals have disappeared, because we have no food to feed them," Cora says. "We have no magic. We cannot save ourselves as we are trying to do. We are dying." The people murmur around her. They, of course, have felt the hands of Death as well. They have felt the empty of their bellies, the hunger that follows them through the streets and inside their doors and into their beds.

"And we must first do something about that," Cora says. "For a people who cannot eat is a people who cannot save."

The people nod. Yes, what she says is true. One cannot think or plan or move when one is stricken by hunger, as the people of Fairendale are.

And now, Cora lets her voice grow hard. "Meanwhile," she says, "the royal family continues living their lives, as if nothing out of the ordinary has happened at all." She lowers her voice, for this is the important part. "They steal from us. So we shall steal from them."

"You mean the prince?" Bertie says.

He always was a sharp man. Cora has known him since they were children. She had thought, once, that she might marry him, after the first man she loved chose to leave, but that was not in her future. She married a sailor, for his easy manner and his long trips away. She preferred living alone, you see.

"And what will that do?" Garron says. "What will that possibly give us? Another mouth to feed?"

"An important mouth to feed," Cora says. "One that will not be ignored."

The people murmur again. Cora lets them and waits until the chatter has died down. "And time," she says. "For if we are fed, if the king calls off his search, we may very well be able to find our children before he does. We may very well be able to save them. We may very well have the right bargaining pawn to restore Fairendale to its former glory."

The people nod. "Yes," they say all around. "Yes."

She knew they would see reason. She knew they would agree, for what parent could not see the opportunity in negotiation? They will not, of course, do to Prince Virgil what the king has done to their children. He will be cared for.

No one says a word about what might happen if they should fail. If the prince escapes. If the king charges them all with treason.

These are wonderings for another day, perhaps.

Or perhaps they are not wonderings that belong in the hearts of parents at all.

The people, before the candle has burned to its bottom, review their plans. Not one of them refuses to follow.

They will do what needs to be done. Or they shall die trying.

The king's men search all morning to find Sir Greyson's sword in the enchanted forest. He thought it unwise to tell the king what they had found and, last eve, merely returned to the castle gates, urging his men to keep their secret safe. They counted heads, and they had only lost one man, a soldier who had urged the rest to go, go, go, and he would take up the rear guard. He did not make it out of the forest, as far as they could tell. When Sir Greyson asked the men who had fled around him, they could not tell what it was they had seen, for they were focused on one purpose only: to get safely out of the woods, away from the dangers that lurked at every turn. And so they did. They rode faster than they have, perhaps, ever ridden in their lives. And the missing man remains a mystery.

The men, last eve, returned to the castle and slept the whole night in fear, and at the first light of dawn, they were up again, entering the woods to see what was left for them. Sir Greyson, truth be told, feels a coward for not remaining in the woods, by his sword, for his men search long and hard, in the direction they were sure they rode as the sun disappeared last eve, but they have found nothing, no sign of his sword, no hint of the children. He does not understand it. If he knew the nature of magic, perhaps he would. Magic, you see, is full of illusions and charm, and one can never know whether what one sees is real or merely a trick of the eye. And so the men say they rode south, but was it, in fact, east? Did they turn to the west? Where was the sun? Where is the sword?

Sir Greyson has nearly given up the search, for there will not be enough daylight left to trace the footsteps they will not be able to see anyway. And then a man gives a shout. Sir Greyson's head snaps in the man's direction. He is waving his captain to him. And there it is, his steel sword, sticking straight from the ground, its hilt pointed toward the dragon lands of Morad. It bobs side to side, as if the footsteps of a giant shake the ground. It does not appear so sturdy as it was last night. Was it moved?

How would they know?

Sir Greyson hails his men. They stand looking at it. "The dragon lands," says Sir Merrick. "We will never find them there. No man is permitted."

"They are not permitted either," Sir Greyson says. "Perhaps we shall find them on the perimeter."

Though the words sound brave, Sir Greyson shivers down deep. He knows the rule of the land, that no man is allowed passage into the dragon lands. And what if the children have crossed the boundary? The king has ordered his men to search everywhere. Will Sir Greyson risk war with dragons to find the children? Sir Greyson has never seen a dragon, but he knows their might. The stories tell of it, though one might agree that stories sometimes do not capture truth so well as they capture fable.

Perhaps the dragons no longer exist. They have not been seen for many, many years, after all. Surely they would have been sighted if they still lived in these lands. Surely someone would have noticed.

Perhaps the stories were only stories, intended to keep children from wandering the woods. Sir Greyson knows, better than most, that stories such as these do not always keep children from the places that are said to hold danger. Sometimes it makes children more inclined to explore them. He himself had ventured into the woods one night when he was just a boy. He had always been curious and brave beyond his years. His mother nearly died at the sight of him emerging from between the trees. She raced straight to him, drawing him out even while he watched eyes lining up in the dark interior of the forest. He did not know to what they belonged. He had seen and felt the danger that night, and that was enough for him. He would never do it again. But what if his mother had not been there?

Sir Greyson and his men gaze at the sky. The sun is marching toward the west, but there is still plenty of daylight left. "We shall go," he says. There are no footsteps for them to follow, and so the only proof they have as to where the steps so clearly led last eve is the direction of his sword. He knows that, without magic, one cannot turn the direction of his hilt once the sword is firmly entrenched in the ground, for the sword Sir Greyson carries is an enchanted one that can only be removed by him or his heir. The old woman might have had magic, but perhaps she did not think to change its direction. She did, after all, point out the footsteps in the first place, as if aiding them in their quest.

Sir Greyson retrieves his sword and slides it back into his scabbard, and then he and his men race through the forest, dodging the thickly positioned trees, racing the sun and the moon and all the dangers of the forest, racing their fear and their hope all in the same moment. They will have to camp in the dragon lands tonight, if there is no clearing, no relief from the forest, for once they reach the edge, there will not be enough light left in the day to ensure they make it back out of the Weeping Woods. Sir Greyson has not yet told his men. Would they continue their quest if they knew? He cannot not be sure. After losing one man to the forest, they all shake at its power.

His men ride, without a single complaint, with hardly a thought, for they are exhausted and desperate to find the children and, finally, rest. They do not consider what finding the children may mean, even the ones who have children of their own, for considering would mean a considerable crisis of decision, and these men only know that they are desperate to finish a quest. When a man has been searching as long as these have, it becomes difficult to remember what is right and what is wrong, what is good and what is evil. You would be surprised, dear reader, at the ways a mind can turn when one is exhausted and desperate.

Sir Greyson, like his men, merely wants an end to this never-ending search. He merely wants to know that life will return to what it once was. He merely sees what is right in front of his face: the approaching end, not the consequences of that end.

So it is that Sir Greyson and his men journey forth with no thought of what the king will do to the poor children they have been charged to capture and deliver. They think only of darkness and only of finishing and only of remaining alive long enough to eat a decent meal and sleep a decent sleep. They think only of doing this task which they have been given.

Rest. It will be so very good to rest.

Perhaps, dear reader, if the king had granted their respite, they might have made a decision that lined up with their ideals, one that would include letting the children escape, but, alas, we shall never know.

The woods grow darker as the men race their horses through it. The fairies begin their flight, dropping every now and again to touch a man on his back, but the men do not turn their faces any which way but the way that is before them. The ground shakes beneath the clap of hooves, and all the other creatures, winged and legged alike, remain hidden. Dusk will come soon, but the creatures of this forest know there is nothing for them in two hundred men racing through trees—nothing, that is, except their own trampled death.

So though there is only one sword that can fend off the creatures of this forest, should they attack, the terror of all the land's stories remain in their tree homes and their underground holes and their secret caves, watching the men pass.

But Sir Greyson and his men must hurry.

Hurry, hurry, hurry.

And so this is what they do, on and on and on, until the sun is barely a shining sliver of gold above the edge of the horizon. It is at this very moment, the moment when the villagers of Fairendale used to look toward the mermaid waters, hoping to see the flash of a tail, that the king's men reach the boundary line between the Weeping Woods and the dragon lands of Morad.

Sir Greyson halts his men. They fan out beside him, until they are two hundred across, for not one of them wants to keep a horse flank in the forest come nightfall. They are tired men, but they are still prudent men. The forest does not spill out of the forest. So they do not spill in. They imagine themselves safe on this small strip of land between two dangers, though they are exposed, for the boundary land is flat and green and wide open.

Sir Greyson dismounts from his horse and toes the imaginary line. "This is it," he says. "This is as far as we may go." His men gaze upon the land. It has not a splash of green or color beyond that of dirt—dusty red and brown and all the shades in between. It is a desolate land. They cannot tear their eyes away from its loneliness, for they feel it in their own hearts.

Sir Greyson looks back at the forest. He looks at the land. And then he looks at his men, who, for a moment, tear their eyes from the fading view before them and meet these of their captain. "We shall camp here this night," Sir Greyson says.

The men dismount. Sir Greyson stills them again with his hand. "They cannot have gone far," he says. "They know the agreement as well as we do. No human is to cross this boundary or they suffer the wrath of the dragons."

"Beg your pardon, Captain," a man in his guard says. He tosses his head toward the dragon lands. "The dragons have left that land."

Sir Greyson squints, peers into the growing dark. "Dragons are very good at hiding," he says. "We cannot know for sure."

A great, long breath whooshes around them. Believe it or not, it is the disappointment of the soldiers. The men, you see, had hoped they might cross into the abandoned dragons lands, find the children, and secure their rest far sooner than now. As it is, they must camp on a small stretch of earth, without blankets or anything of comfort but their own metal armor, which, as I am sure we might all agree, does not lend them the slightest bit of warmth.

"And what shall we do here?" another man calls out.

"We shall camp," Sir Greyson says. "And keep a diligent watch. We will find them if they are here."

Our captain of the king's guard tries to sound hopeful, though it is difficult even for him. Instead, his eyes appear as tired as those of his men, with a small fleck of sorrow. He is so very sorry for them. He is so very sorry for himself.

But the men do not complain. They merely stretch out their bodies, beneath the bellies of their horses, clad in their full armor, which grows colder by the minute, and try to sleep. Most of them do not, of course. So rather than having one watch man on duty every two hours, there are, in fact, two hundred.

And the only one grateful for this unexpected help is the one assigned to the watch, for he knows he is not alone.

These men are afraid, you see. And can we blame them? In these hours between riding through an enchanted wood and reaching a dangerous dragon land, they have become like children once more, terrified by the stories their parents told them when they were younger. They are supposed to be brave and strong. They are not supposed to be little children shaking in their armor, every turn of the wind bringing terror up to their throats.

We know, dear reader, that bravery is not the absence of fear but is, instead, facing your fear. The king's men will learn this soon enough.

For now, let us leave them where they lie and hope they may find a little sleep, for there is a great adventure coming on the morrow.

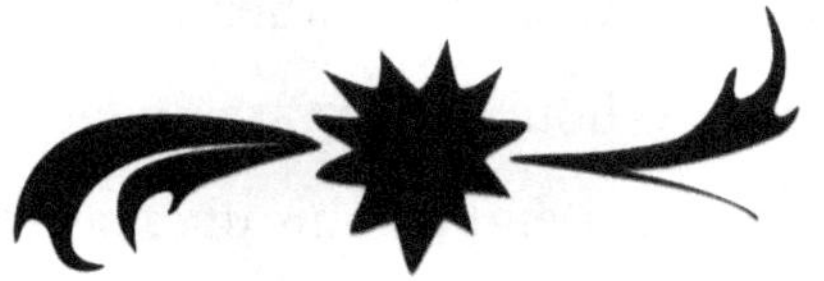

Peace

One day, when Cora was still a girl of seven, the village erupted in a roar.

The king, it seemed, had banished his son, the one who stole to the village at night and provided food for the hungry and blankets for the cold. The only good-hearted man among the men of King Sebastien's castle, banished for the very reason the villagers loved him: his kindness.

The village people were outraged. They stormed through the streets and into the center of town, and they gathered at the fountain but did not dare open the underground chamber. They cursed their king.

Cora's father found her among the villagers in the streets. He had come with news of his own, but when he saw the people cursing in the streets, he raised his voice and his hands and said, "People of Fairendale," and every head turned his way. "Listen to me, please." They looked at him and he looked at them. His eyes softened. Their eyes softened. "I beg you," he said. "We must keep the peace. At all costs."

A few of the village men, known for their tempers, shouted at him and called him mad. But the fire had gone out of the others, for they respected Cora's father as an advisor of sorts. He had always shown himself to be a wise man, and a kind one, too.

"How will we keep the peace?" one of the men shouted. His face turned red like the flowers that sprinkled the hill. "The king has stolen our help. Our children will starve."

"We will find a way," Cora's father said. "We will plant a garden, perhaps."

The angry men grumbled, but a woman spoke up. "I tended a garden as a girl." She was a woman who had not been born in Fairendale, but one who had followed her husband when he met her on his travels.

The fire, however, had not cooled in Cora. She found herself protesting. "From what will we plant a garden, Father? We have nothing left."

Her father looked at her, his eyes wide in that way he had when he was surprised, or, perhaps, disappointed. He had not expected her to thwart his peace efforts, you see. But she could not support his peace, now, could she? The king had banished the only goodness in the castle. They could not live without goodness. A world cannot survive without goodness.

They must fight back. They must let the king know that he could not banish a man who had saved them from starvation. They could not simply die and do nothing about their dying.

"We will make do," Cora's father said.

"With what, Father?" Cora said, louder this time, for she wanted the people to hear. She wanted their fight. "With what will we make do?" She spread her hands before her and then waved them back toward the village houses. "There is nothing left."

And though she was only a girl of seven, the townspeople looked at her, and they saw the truth. Cora found that she could be powerful with not only her magic but also her words. She felt the power in her hands, and she held it and turned it over and kept it until the time was right to let it loose.

"My daughter," her father said. He looked around at the people. They had eyes only for Cora. "She has the magic that can do this. She can save us." He turned back to Cora.

Cora did not quite expect to become the savior. She looked at the power in her hands and then shook her head. "No, Father," she said. "I cannot create something from nothing. Without Prince Wendell's gifts from the castle, we will not make enough food. There is nothing we do not need. Nothing we can use to turn into food."

"So we will gather what we do not need," her father said. He held up a finger. "Stay here for a moment." He walked toward their cottage and disappeared inside. When he came back out he was carrying a blanket that used to be her mother's, a blanket neither of them had touched since her mother died.

Her father held it out to her. "Here," he said. "We do not need this." His eyes were darker than the forest trees. She knew it was sorrow that turned them so.

"No, Father," Cora said. She turned away. She could not bear to see the blanket in his hands, to imagine it gone from the chair where her mother used to sit.

Her father's eyes turned glassy. "I will do whatever it takes to see that you eat."

"Not this, Father," Cora said. Her throat felt tight and heavy. "I will not do this."

Her father shook the blanket, his eyes spilling now. "We do not need it," he said. His voice rose in desperation. "Do it, Cora."

"No," she said, and the wind picked up with her voice.

Her father grabbed her by the arms and shook her. She could not feel the power any longer, not with her father's hands and the shaking and the way she could not think.

There were noises all around her, and when Cora looked, the people had gathered a small pile of candelabras and silverware and bowls, what they did not absolutely need. Cora shook her head.

"See?" her father said. "Do you see, Cora? We will find a way."

"It is a bandage," Cora said. "Nothing more."

"But it is enough," her father said. "For now."

Cora looked back at the people. "We must find the root," she said. Her voice grew louder again. "We must pull it out."

The people looked at her with sad eyes. Her father turned her toward him again. "No," he said. "We must keep peace. We must be good people."

"Good people do not give in to bad people," she said.

Her father's shoulders drew forward nearly imperceptibly, though Cora noticed, for she knew her father well. "My daughter," he said. "You have much to learn." And then he leaned closer, and his voice grew softer, barely more than a whisper. "Good people wait for the right time. The time is not now."

And so, because she loved her father, and because she loved the people of this village, she did it. She turned their offerings into a garden. And she made it flourish with enough food for the people to eat modestly well. They did not always sleep with full bellies, that much is true, but they did not starve.

Cora performed her magic quietly, waiting for the right time.

Always waiting for the right time.

Arrival

Prince Virgil sits in his room, alone. The sun is setting, he knows, somewhere outside the castle walls, but he has no interest in seeing its display. He has not had interest in it since the children disappeared, for the sun no longer drifts away to beauty and warmth, only shadow and cold. It has no one to admire it anymore, you see, so why should it try? Prince Virgil knows that he would have admired it well enough, but one boy is not an audience, is it, dear reader?

Tonight, Prince Virgil sits alone, missing his friends. He misses tearing through the streets with them and watching the eyes of Mercy, dancing green like the grass waving in wind, and he misses laughing at Hazel with her pretty blue eyes and the way she could turn anything around to a game. He could use a game right now, to take his mind off this endless pursuit his father has chosen.

Mostly, though, he misses his best friend. He does not want to remember the last day he saw Theo. He was horrid to his friend, and this is not the memory he would like to keep of their time together, though it is the only one that visits him anymore. He would like to remember the time before those last days, when Theo took him out to his father's work shed, which had stacks and stacks of wood in corners and across a large table. Prince Virgil remembers seeing, that day, a collection of wood laid out like a table, unfinished, for someone in the village, perhaps. Prince Virgil wonders if the table still exists, unfinished, with no one in the village to need it.

His father, in the last days, has broken two of the royal dining room chairs. Prince Virgil had seen his father break one this eve, a mighty crack sounding through the room and startling the servants. Prince Virgil, in truth, had to work very hard not to laugh at the sight of it—his father lying on his back, unable to get back on his feet. It took three servants to pick him up again.

They had no Arthur to fix those chairs. When they were all broken, what would they do? The king would, perhaps, eat while sitting on his throne. Those who dined with him, which was usually no one but, on occasion now, Prince Virgil, would sit at his feet, as the king preferred his inferiors.

Prince Virgil had overheard the servants whispering about the king, that he was growing much too fat and soon would need a throne of special order from the land of the giants. Prince Virgil's ears burned to hear his father spoken of like this, but he did not correct them, merely went on his own way. He did not want to make more enemies than he had in the castle.

A boy of twelve, with enemies, you might ask? How could this be?

Well, you see, it is not entirely correct to say that Prince Virgil has enemies for any reason other than the fact that he is the king's son. Not many within the castle, alas, love King Willis. By extension, not many love Prince Virgil, though it must be said that the servants love their dear Queen Clarion. Perhaps if the prince spent more time with his mother. Perhaps if he called them by their proper names. Perhaps if he showed them a shred of his sorrow, they would love him as they did his mother.

Just before retiring to his chambers this eve, Prince Virgil had sat on the throne, at his father's behest. The throne, it seemed, preferred him to remember the last day he had seen Theo and so had lobbed the memory at him over and over again, until Prince Virgil could do nothing more than fly from his seat and out the doors, unable to hear his father calling after him. The words that chased him to his bedchamber were the last ones Theo had said to him—that he would not want the throne even if he did have magic (which he had lied about, by the way. Prince Virgil cannot forgive this just yet).

So it is that Prince Virgil is shut behind his door, hiding away from the sun's setting that is not really a sun's setting at all, but like one glowing cloud that fades as quickly as it caught on fire. So it is that he thinks, desperately, of another day, a better day, when Theo brought him to the corner of Arthur's shop, where a crate of wood touched the wall. That day, Theo rummaged through the scraps and pulled out a small box.

"I made this for you," he had said, staring at the ground. He handed the box to Prince Virgil. "For your birthday. It is not much, but…"

Prince Virgil had turned the wooden box over and over in his hands. On the top was carved *Prince Virgil* and the crest of the kingdom, a ferocious bear bordered by elegant flourishes. On the bottom was a message. *To my best friend.* He could not, at the time, imagine how long it had taken his friend to make a treasure such as that one, and the thought of days and days spent carving and smoothing was what made Prince Virgil hug Theo as he had never done before. Theo, surprised, had hugged him back.

The memory shifts. He remembers Theo looking at the floor, saying he made that beautiful box for Prince Virgil. But why would he look at the floor? Was he lying? Did he have something to hide?

The throne, you see, has made its mark on Prince Virgil,

even in the short time he has been sitting on its golden seat. The light, even now, wrestles with the dark, though he is far away from it inside his bedchambers. The memory grows dark. He sees his friend lying. He sees his friend using magic instead of the carving knife he used to whittle scraps of his father's wood into figures. He sees only what the darkness wants him to see.

And this is what pulls Prince Virgil from his bed, what carries him to the keepsake box, what flings it from his hands onto the marble floor. He watches it shatter, splinters and wood shards flying all beneath the furniture that Arthur built.

Prince Virgil collapses to the floor. It is the first time he has cried since his friends disappeared, since he told their secret, since he decided the throne was better than companionship. And oh, dear reader, how he regrets it. He gathers the splinters toward him, unaware of the way they cut the skin on his hands. He wishes he had not broken this box. It is all that remains of his friend. He touches the talisman around his neck. No. Not all that remains. But this box was touched lovingly by Theo. Why did he break what his friend had touched?

His friend was never his friend in the first place. Prince Virgil flings the pieces away once more.

But this is Theo's work, made for him. Prince Virgil gathers them up.

He was no friend. Prince Virgil flings them away.

This is how Queen Clarion finds her son when she comes in to bid him goodnight. He is curled up on the floor, grasping the wood in both his hands, begging to keep them.

"My son," she says. She rushes to his side and kneels before him. Her skirts brush pieces of wood. "Whatever is the matter?"

Prince Virgil does not want to talk about it. So he says nothing.

Queen Clarion takes her son in her arms. She pulls him to his feet and leads him to his bed. "You are tired, my dear," she says. "You must get some rest." She touches his bandage, her hand trailing his cheek.

Prince Virgil permits her to tuck him beneath the blankets. Queen Clarion sits on the side of his bed, examining his hands. "Your hands," she says. She looks toward the broken box. "The wood."

Prince Virgil finally speaks. "It does not hurt," he says, though, in truth, it does. It hurts quite a bit, the wood pieces lodged in his hands, tiny little ones that would take a seeing glass to extract. But it is the price one must pay for betrayal. So he does not say a word about them.

"I will summon Calvin," Queen Clarion says, rising from the bed. "He is skilled in healing, I have heard."

"No," Prince Virgil says. "Please, Mother, tell me a story."

Queen Clarion hesitates for a moment, though she loves

stories as much as her boy does. But his hands. His rest. She sits on the side of the bed again, unable to resist this request from her son. She has told him all sorts of stories over the years—but there was one she had not dared tell him.

Perhaps it is time.

She has, after all, seen her son sitting on the throne. She has seen him wrestling with the light and the dark. She has seen the mark it has laid upon him, and she must, now, tell of another who could not escape its hold.

So she begins her story. "Once upon a time," she says, "in a land far away, there lived a brave prince." She looks at her son. "He looked quite a bit like you, my son. Handsome. Kind. Strong of heart and love. But he had an evil father."

Thus she weaves her tale, so skillfully Prince Virgil does not know how much of it is true. So he asks.

"It was a true story?" he says.

Queen Clarion dips her head. She has woven the truth into a story, but she does not know if she wants to tell him this or if she would rather have him come to his own conclusions. But she decides it is best to tell the truth. "Yes," she says. "Yes, it is a true story. Your grandfather, King Sebastien..."

She does not finish, but Prince Virgil pieces it together. "So he died from the wounds of a blackbird," he says. The story, you see, told of an evil king who had been blinded by a blackbird.

"Not immediately," Queen Clarion says. "We do not know if he died from the blackbird's attack or whether it was something else entirely."

"What else might it have been?" Prince Virgil says, though, if you remember, his mother has told him once before.

"Heart sickness," Queen Clarion says. "As we suspect."

"But he was attacked by a blackbird," Prince Virgil says. He shivers.

"Yes," Queen Clarion says.

"Why would a blackbird attack my grandfather?" Prince Virgil says.

Queen Clarion looks at her son, sees his pale face and his sad eyes and the curly hair gathered around his cheeks. The fire's glow softens the hard lines of his face, making him appear more boy than young man. "In this land," she says, "blackbirds are known for seeking out evil."

"And destroying it?" Prince Virgil says.

"If they are permitted," Queen Clarion says.

"And someone permitted my grandfather's death?" Prince Virgil says.

"It was done on a dark night," Queen Clarion says. "No one knew." She does not meet her son's eyes, as if there are more secrets left for another day. Of course there are always more secrets, dear reader. One does not often learn the whole truth in one moment or story.

"Was the bird caught?" Prince Virgil says.

Queen Clarion stares into the fire. Her eyes dance with flames, yellow sparks licking her blue. "No," she says. "The bird never came back after it had finished with your grandfather."

"And do you think it lives still?" Prince Virgil says, for, as one might expect, he is a bit worried about this blackbird. He did not realize they were so dangerous.

"Perhaps," Queen Clarion says. "But you do not have to worry over such things." She touches her son's hand and smiles. "You are not evil, my son."

Prince Virgil does not say anything for a long while. He has seen the darkness in his own heart. He knows it lives there. What if a blackbird finds him? What if it sees the evil, too? And because a wondering so large as this cannot be contained in one single body, Prince Virgil speaks his words aloud. "What if I am evil, too?"

"Oh, my child," Queen Clarion says. She enfolds her son in the warmth of her arms, and he feels the light of her spread to his chest and settle there. "You are nothing like your grandfather." She kisses the top of his head. "Nothing."

He pulls away from her. "But what if I am?" he says, for now he has another wondering, and sometimes, dear reader, we just need to know that we will still be loved, regardless of the darkness that may live in us. Prince Virgil knows this need well. His father loves only the dark. Does his mother love only the light? Will he have to choose between the love of one and the love of another?

Queen Clarion rests her hand on the side of his face, and she does not take her eyes from his. "I will love you no matter who you decide to be," she says. "No matter what you do or have done or will do. No matter where you go."

Oh, the gift of words such as these. For a moment Prince Virgil can see only light, reaching from his mother's eyes to his own, and then he can feel the warmth of goodness shifting through him. He feels fuller.

And he knows that he does not have to worry about a blackbird that once pecked the life out of his grandfather. Because he is made of both dark and light, and this night, he has chosen light.

Perhaps it will not always be so, but it is this night.

Queen Clarion rises from Prince Virgil's bed and kisses her son's head once more. She hovers in the doorway to watch him settle onto his back, close his eyes and fall into a deep and dreamless sleep.

She smiles to herself and shuts his door.

Maude is growing restless. Arthur has ventured out once more, though now, when she looks from the mouth of the cave, she can see the armor of an army flashing in the light of the moon. She knows the men have found them, and where there are king's men, there is grave danger for the children. So she waits. And fidgets. And waits. Every now and again, she rises from her place at the head of her daughter, who sleeps like all the other children, and peers out once more. Arthur has been gone much longer than he has ever been gone. Before he slipped out this time, he told her that he would search for more water, but it was not likely that the dragon's land had much water at all beyond the first drying-up pool he found. Arthur believes the dragons have left, that all the nourishment the land used to hold has dried up. Maude, though, has always been the more practical of the two. She would rather proceed through the land with great caution, as if the dragons still live here, rather than great recklessness, to which Arthur, as long as she has known him, has been prone.

Arthur delivered to her that bit of news, the bit about the dragons no longer living here, with great disappointment, though Maude could not for the life of her understand why dragons abandoning a land they must cross with all these children would come as a disappointment to her husband, before announcing, in a whisper that would not wake the sleeping children, that he must locate more water, for they had run out of their last stores and were, even now, breathing through the driest mouths they had ever tasted. She had agreed, for she knew they could not live long in a world without water.

But now that Arthur has gone missing, Maude is not so sure she should have let him out. If he does not return, how would she get the children across the land on her own, with the king's men watching? How would she save them? They would not survive in a cave. How long would the king's men wait?

Might she take the children elsewhere? She does not know these lands as Arthur does, but perhaps…

She cannot think on this. She peers into the dark, but there is nothing to indicate that her husband has been discovered, which is cause for relief, or returned, which is cause for fear.

Her belly rumbles. Somewhere a child stirs. They have only eaten old dried-out leaves in this land, for it does not hold much life and the children no longer hold much magic. They have lost the strongest among them. They have grown too hungry, too thirsty, to channel their gift.

And Hazel. Maude has not dared ask if Hazel has felt her gift drain from her veins, for she cannot know, yet, what has happened to her dear Theo, not while they all still face danger.

Maude shivers. The land has grown colder even in the few

hours they have slept in the cave. They must journey north, to temperatures even colder than this. They are ill prepared. They will never make it.

Our dear Maude has momentarily forgotten how to hope. She needs Arthur for this, too. But Arthur does not come. She is left only with starving children and shallow breaths and the king's men lined up outside the mouth of the cave, waiting.

Were we to see Arthur, we would know, as Maude cannot, that the reason for his delay is that he has ventured much farther than he has ever gone before. He must, for there are no more leaves. There is only dirt, and I am sure you will agree that children cannot eat dirt. But he has come upon a small stream in the center of the land, only a trickle, but flowing still, and so he bends and tries to fill the jug, again and again and again until he has a few drops that might be spread among the children, to sustain them for another day.

The jug is not heavy on his return, though Arthur is more bones than flesh now. But hope sustains him. They will leave on the morrow, and they will make it to the stream at midday, and the children will be able to drink as long as they wish. He will make sure of that.

A flash turns his head toward the Weeping Woods. What is it, catching the light of the moon? He squints, stretches his neck, but it is impossible to see, for clouds creep over the moon now. If he cannot see it, perhaps it cannot see him. Still, he moves silently, slowly, taking cover behind rocks that nearly hide him in his entirety.

It takes him much longer to reach the mouth of the cave than he intends. Maude sleeps, her back slumped against the wall.

"Dear Maude," he whispers when he reaches her and crouches before her form. He takes her hands, and she startles awake.

"Arthur," Maude says, her eyes wide. She pulls him to her, and he nearly crashes into the wall. "I thought we had lost you."

Arthur pulls back. "I found more water," he says. He nearly laughs himself silly with the news of it. "In the middle of the land." He holds the jug up for her to see. She peers in, and though it is dark, it is plain to see that not much water sits in the bottom. But Maude does not say anything.

"Shall we wake the children?" Arthur says. He looks behind her, though darkness covers the sleeping ones.

"No," Maude says. "It will be morning soon enough."

"We shall leave at first light," Arthur says. "We will make it to the water by midday."

"Arthur—" Maude says, but Arthur is still laying out his plan.

"The water should carry us through the remainder of the

land, if we are careful. And then we shall be back in lands of food and water and opportunity." Arthur grabs Maude's hand and brings it to his lips. "No more than three days' journey, if I remember correctly."

"Perhaps you did not see them," Maude says, as if speaking to herself. Her voice grows soft, hardly a whisper.

"See what?" Arthur says.

Maude looks at her husband. Her eyes turn glassy and soft. "The king's men."

"The king's men?" Arthur says. A child stirs, and he and Maude wait until the breathing has evened again. The poor children. They are so very tired.

"They are right outside the boundary," Maude says. "They are too close to us."

Arthur rocks back on his heels. "No," he says.

"They arrived while you were out searching for food," Maude says. She does not ask if he found food, though her stomach wants nothing more than something to fill it.

"I saw something," Arthur says.

"You saw them?" Maude says.

"No," Arthur says. "Just a gleam of something. The moon is gone."

"Might they have seen you?" Maude says.

"No," Arthur says. "It is too dark."

They do not speak for some time, both thinking about the trap in which they have stepped.

"I heard the ground shake," Maude says. "Earlier this eve."

"As did I," Arthur says. He had thought the shaking meant dragons, but nothing showed itself, and so he had chalked it up to his own imagination.

"I should have taken the children and followed you," Maude says.

"You did not know," Arthur says. He pulls Maude toward him. She lays her head on his shoulder.

"Whatever will we do, Arthur?" Maude says, for the hopelessness has climbed from the back of her throat out into words. And Arthur, alas, cannot say, for it matters not when they choose to leave, they will be spotted by the king's men.

"We must risk it," Arthur says. "We must leave here as soon as we can."

"They will see us," Maude says. "We will not be able to escape."

"Perhaps there is still hope," Arthur says. "Perhaps there are still dragons."

Maude pulls away and studies Arthur's face, though it is far too dark to see. "Dragons? Yet another danger."

"Perhaps," Arthur says. "Perhaps not."

Maude narrows her eyes, though the narrowing is lost on

Arthur. "What would you know of dragons that leads you to believe they are no danger?" she says.

"I studied dragons for a time," Arthur says, closing his eyes. "I knew them quite well."

Maude knows that Arthur is tired, so she lets it go at that. But there is one more thing she must say, and it is this: "We should have left as soon as we arrived here."

"Perhaps," Arthur says. "One cannot always tell the future." He rubs Maude's arm. "When one is not a prophet."

Why is it that Maude and Arthur never became prophets in their time? For the ability is offered to all sorcerers, just before their first child receives the gift of magic. Well, dear reader, we must not get ahead of ourselves. That is a story for another time. For now, we must note that both Arthur and Maude regret, if only for a moment, that they did not agree to the terms.

"If only," Maude says.

Arthur takes her hand once more. "We cannot dwell on what is already done, only on what must be done," he says. Arthur is a wise man, would you not agree? Of course one should not dwell on what is already done, for not a thing can be done to change it. We are only permitted to change the future.

Maude nods her head, but, in truth, she is thinking, even now, about Fairendale and its loveliness, the home she shared with Theo and Hazel and Arthur, the friends who gathered in the streets every eve to watch the sun's setting. She misses her home. She misses her friends. She misses her son.

"We shall leave in the early morn," Arthur says now.

"But the king's men will surely see us," Maude says.

Arthur nods. "Yes," he says. "They will see us."

Maude waits for him to speak, and when he does not, because he has fallen asleep in the middle of a thought, she says, "So we will be captured."

"No," Arthur says. "The king's men will not cross into the lands."

"You cannot be sure of that," Maude says.

"No," Arthur says again. "But I hope."

And so Maude, who is not so easily given to optimism, chooses to hope as well.

They drift off to sleep together, sitting with their backs against the cave walls, their heads propped against one another, waiting for the morning's first light.

Opportunity

Cora's father never moved. Months passed. Cora turned eight, then nine, then ten, then fifteen. Every morning her father would walk to the castle before she woke and return after she had gone to bed. She hardly saw him anymore.

One night, though, she stayed up late to see him, just for a moment.

He walked into their home and startled. "Cora," he said. "I did not expect to see you."

"What is it, Father?" she said. "What is it that keeps you so long at the castle?" She pulled out her father's chair, where a bowl of soup had grown cold. He sat and picked up his spoon.

"Thank you, my dear, for cooking," he said. He looked up at her, and his eyes were so very sad that she could not bear to see. She turned away while he said, "I should be cooking."

She waited for him to eat what little there was, and then she asked her question again.

"The king," her father said. "He has demanded more hours and more responsibilities. I have only just finished."

"What responsibilities?" Cora said.

"Securing the food," her father said. "The king must ensure that no food leaves the castle."

"But no one from the castle even comes to the village anymore," Cora said. "Not since King Wendell was banished."

Her father raised his eyes to hers again. "I do," he said, and the words held a thousand regrets.

"But you do not bring food," Cora said. "Do you, Father?"

Her father did not answer. He stared at his soup, which was only broth now.

"What do they do with all the extra food, Father?" Cora said.

"It is time for sleep," her father said, rising from his chair. "I am very tired."

"But what do they do with it?" Cora said.

Her father shook his head. "Must you know?"

"Yes," Cora said. "I will not let you rest until I know." She smiled, but her father did not smile back at her.

"They dump it," he said. "In a heap pile beyond the castle."

"Where we might collect it?" Cora said. An idea warmed her chest. There might yet be a way.

Her father shook his head again. "No," he said. "There are guards. Many of them. You would never make it out alive."

But she would. She knew a way, you see. And so one night she tried. She slipped into her feathers and flew in the dark of night with the biggest basket she could carry in her beak. She landed on a wall and watched the guards, memorizing their movements. And then she made her move.

She filled up the basket as quickly as she could, and then she disappeared. She dropped the offerings at the doors of the people, and, come morning, they were gone.

Over time, she grew stronger and was able to carry a larger basket. Back and forth, back and forth she flew. Before long, the people had called the feast waiting at their doors a miracle of the most magical kind.

Until, one night, she was discovered.

It was a new guard, who did not keep the same rhythm as the others. She had been careless, not wasting precious time to watch where he walked.

"Hey," the guard said, as if he knew exactly what she was. "Shoo." It took him a moment to notice the basket in her beak. She took to the sky before he could reach her, but she knew that he had seen what mattered most.

The next evening there were six guards, one on each side, stationed there, and two who roamed, and she flew over the great heap and did not stop. The people had no leftover roast lamb the following day. And the next evening was the same. And the eve after that, the king stood waiting.

"There," a guard said. "There it is." He pointed to the sky, to her.

"Blackbirds do not venture this close to humans," the king said, "It is no place for them."

"Perhaps it is hungry," another guard said.

The king squinted up at her. She saw her chance. She made her calculations. And then she dove.

The king's scream was heard all the way back in the village of Fairendale. It took only seconds to gouge out his eyes, and then he was writhing on the ground, and the men knelt beside the king and tried to staunch the blood, but she had already taken flight. They looked up at the sky, and then they looked back at their king, with no eyes and a blood-stained face, and they drew their weapons, for they knew then that this was no ordinary blackbird. They chased Cora as long as they dared, but she flew into the Weeping Woods, and they did not follow.

Cora, though, did not return home. She saw another opportunity, for she had drawn the king's men far away from the side of the one they had sworn to protect, and so she returned for one last attack.

Her hate, you see, had become dark and sinister, and the

kingdom, in her eyes, was better off without a man such as this one ruling it.

When she took flight again, she did not know if she finished the job. But she returned to her father's house and waited for him to return as well.

He came hours later. She was still up waiting, sitting by the fire, staring into it.

"Cora," her father said. "My dear, it is very late."

"I could not sleep," she said.

Her father looked at her. His eyes were sad. "The king," he said. "He was attacked tonight."

Why would her father feel sad about a man like the king getting what he most deserved? Cora felt only relief.

"Attacked?" Cora said, though the only question she wanted to ask was whether or not he was alive.

"Yes," her father said. "By a blackbird." He looked at his daughter long and hard. He did not know about her shape shifting. No one did. This was a secret Cora had kept from the world, though if her mother had been alive, she would have guessed, for Cora's mother had been a shape shifter in her time.

"How very strange," Cora said. A hardness crept into her voice. "And does he live?"

"Yes," her father said. "Barely."

So she had not finished the job. She felt the disappointment of regret.

"The healer says he will not live the morrow," Cora's father said.

"How very sad," Cora said.

Her father still gazed at her. Perhaps he had guessed. "A blackbird," he said. "A blackbird who pecked out the eyes of the king and left him to die." He knew about her mother. He had seen her transform once. He had never asked about it, but he had known.

"If he dies," Cora said. "What will happen?"

Her father drew a long breath and then let it loose. The fire flickered on his face. She noticed new wrinkles. He looked much older than he used to.

"Prince Willis will take over," her father said. "And we hope for better." He rose and kissed the top of her head and then disappeared into the room he used to share with her mother.

Cora remained staring at the fire until just before dawn.

Found

It is morning. They have survived the night. They are alive. The king's men look around at one another. They count. They count again. They count once more, and not a one of them has been lost. They let loose a raucous cheer, and in the stillness of early morning, it is thunderous.

"It must have been the boundary line," Sir Greyson says. "Perhaps no harm can come to us on the boundary line." The captain feels good enough to grin at all his men, but, then, what kind of captain grins at his men? So he pulls his helmet over his head so they cannot see the joy in his eyes or the way it stretches across his face. He looks through the slit of his steel, toward the dragon lands. This will be no way to watch. He will have to remove the helmet, but, for now, he keeps the helmet low, his face hidden. No sense in riling up his men with false hope. They do not yet know if they will find anything, least of all the missing children.

But they have survived the night. This is enough hope on its own.

Sir Greyson and his men watch and wait, all four hundred eyes trained toward the wide expanse of dragon lands, looking for a sign that something lives there. The sun is hidden this early morning, so the land stretches before them, bathed in a harsh grey that makes it difficult to see into the distance. But with so many eyes trained on the land, it would be impossible for so many to escape without being discovered, and so Sir Greyson and his men continue their waiting and watching. They hardly dare to blink.

"They will not hide for long," Sir Merrick says. "They will have to search for food. No one can survive without food."

The words send a sharp pain to Sir Greyson's stomach. His men have not been eating as they should. Truth be told, they stand, but they are weak on their feet. They did not bring adequate supplies to camp, and even now, they are longing for the castle grounds, where at least they could pull from the royal garden and fish in the tributary.

"Yes," Sir Greyson says, though his voice is quiet and muffled behind his helmet. "Yes, we will find them soon."

And then, just as the sky lightens to a softer gray, there is movement from a cave in the center of the dragon lands, and one of the men, who was looking that way quite by accident, for he did not think one would travel so far into the dragon lands and live, sees it. It was the head of a man, he is sure. And there it is again, scanning the land. The soldier cries out. He points.

"There!" he says. "There is a man!"

Not one of them knows whether this one man means anything at all, but you must understand that, after so long searching, anything is something. The man appears not to see the king's men and, in their plain view, steps out of the cave. He is alone. He stands alone. He faces them, and they are, for once, glad there is no sun, for they are sure that their armor blends in with the sky. And perhaps it would, dear reader, if they had been standing against the sky. But they are standing against the backdrop of a forest, green everywhere, and so their silver armor stands out most obviously. Still the man remains, turned toward them. Still the man beckons behind him. Still the children come tumbling out.

"What is that?" a man shouts.

"It appears to be children," Sir Greyson says. "A multitude of children."

The men give another cheer, for they know this means, finally, miraculously, an end to their quest and a return to their homes. They have waited so very long for this day, and even Sir Greyson cannot help lifting up a shout of relief.

Finally. Finally they have found that for which they had searched.

Their cheer races across the land, as if it has wings. The trees behind them shake in their own silent cheer. Even the sun, for a moment, bursts through its clouds, disappearing as suddenly as it appeared.

It is as if every moment has led them here.

Sir Greyson cannot help but cry.

Arthur stops mid-step. The cheer has reached his ears. He turns toward the sound. He, of course, knew they were there, but he supposed they would not try to cross the land. And, indeed, the king's men remain where they are, as they are. A whole line of men stands still, like the trees behind them, holding the reins of their horses.

"There," he says. "See, children? Nothing to be afraid of."

At the sound of his voice, Maude and the children turn around. They see what Arthur has seen, and all of them give a gasp in the same collective breath, for they do not see nothing to be afraid of at all. They see the king's men, come to round them up once more. They see dungeons and darkness and danger. They taste fear. What will they do now? If they run, the dragons might sense their heavier foot falls. And yet, the king's men are right behind them.

"Tell them," Maude says, sensing the children's fear. They cannot, in truth, move. They simply stare at the line of men before them.

"They will not cross the boundary," Arthur says. "They will not risk it." He nods toward the men. "You see? They have not moved."

"How far until we reach the end of these dragon lands?" Hazel says. It is a whisper, for though her father has assured them the king's men would not dare cross the boundary line, she cannot feel so sure.

"Three days' journey, at least," Arthur says, for he knows his daughter. He knows her worries, but he tries to remain calm himself. "We must walk, not run. We must take what caution we can."

"They have horses," Chester calls out. "They will surely awaken the dragons."

"They will not cross," Arthur says. And, indeed, the king's men have not yet crossed, still. They would have crossed if they wanted. Arthur's mind moves to what he knows of the dragon lands. They will have to take a straight shot, rather than walk the perimeter, for it would not take nearly so long to cut directly across Morad.

Arthur looks behind him, toward the way they must go. Surely, if the dragons still lived, they would have shown themselves by now. He looks back toward the men. The better way, the less dangerous way, would be to surrender to the king's men. They would hatch a plan of escape then. But the dragons would leave no survivors, should there be any left. It is a great risk.

What seals the decision for him is the rumbling of a child's belly. He knows that the children are not strong enough to escape from the king's guard. They would have to risk. They would have to venture forward.

Hazel gasps. The king's men have moved. They have climbed onto their horses. They look as though they are ready to cross the boundary line.

"Father," she says. Her voice holds all the fears a girl could ever carry.

"Arthur?" Maude says. "We must do something."

"What must we do, Father?" Hazel says. "They are coming. They will cross."

"Run?" Maude says. She looks at her husband, but he does not meet her eye. In the distance, the king's men wait on their commander's order.

"Run," Arthur says.

But before they can even put one foot in front of the other, the whole land gives a violent shake. Once, twice, a thousand times. Arthur stares at his feet, and then, slowly, slowly, slowly he turns around.

He does not need to look to know what he will find.

Sir Greyson watches them watch his men. He wonders why they do not run. He wonders why he does not order his men to attack. He wonders why the whole world holds still, as if they are all frozen into this scene of relief and, on the part of the children and the man, fear.

And then he sees them coming, and he understands. For he, too, had seen the armored man who crossed the boundary line before mounting his horse, the man who had misjudged the distance necessary to swing his leg, the man who had landed heavily back on the ground, one toe across the boundary line. He, too, had held his breath and waited.

Waited for exactly this.

Arthur and Maude and the children are paralyzed, it seems. Not because the only one of them who has seen a living dragon is Arthur, but because they never expected to see so many. Dragons stretch out as far as the eye can see. In fact, there are no more mountains on this land. There are only dragons, and more dragons, and more dragons still.

There are so many dragons. They stand before Arthur and Maude and the children in all their majesty, in all their shimmering elegance, in all their breathtaking menace.

No one will make it out of this alive. They are sure of this.

The dragons line up like the king's men. Men lining one side, dragons lining the other. Maude, Arthur and the children are caught in the very middle of the dangers. They freeze. They cannot lift their feet. They can go nowhere, because they cannot, in truth, feel their legs, which have grown cold and useless in these last moments. Maude has lost all feeling in her face. Hazel does not feel her father's hand move to hers.

The eyes of the dragons glow. They are yellow and red and green and blue and orange and white. They are every color and shade you can imagine, and while one might think it would be a beautiful thing to stare upon so many colors, when those colors are held in the eyes of dragons, it is anything but beautiful.

It does not take an expert on dragons to know that these dragons who stand before Arthur and Maude and all the children, are angry. They are angrier, perhaps, than any other dragons have ever been, for a dragon takes his word seriously.

Years ago these dragons gave their word, and now it is the humans who have betrayed it. No man was supposed to cross into the lands of Morad, just as no dragons were to cross into the land of Fairendale, and now here they are, men and women and children touching the sacred sands of Morad.

One of the dragons, larger than the rest, moves forward. The ground rumbles, but it is nothing to the rumbling in his throat, where his scales turn ivory. Most of him is green, though not all of him. He lowers his head, and the children can see the sharp ivory horns at the top of his head.

"Zorag," Arthur says, but no one is listening.

The dragon glares upon the intruders with golden eyes. His wings are held close to his body, though Arthur knows that those wings could wipe out the king's men in one flap.

The children take a step back, afraid of the eyes that look as if lightning lives in them.

"You dare come into our lands," the dragon says.

Arthur holds up his hands. "Please," he says. "We are in need of escape. This was the only way."

The dragon's head moves up and back, as if he is tasting the clouds that gather in the sky. He lets out a frightful roar that makes the horses in the distance whinny and buck. The horses, you see, would like nothing more than to flee from this dragon danger, but they are well trained and will not go unless their riders permit them. And the riders, truth be told, are frozen in fear, just like the children.

"We made an agreement, long ago," says the dragon, who is the leader in this land, though the humans do not know it. The only clue is his size, for he is much larger than the rest. But the children are too terrified to notice. The dragons all appear large. In fact, the word the children might use to describe these dragons before them is monstrous.

"Yes," Arthur says. "Yes, we know. You are…" Arthur does not finish, though the dragon seems to know what it is Arthur is asking.

"I am called Zorag," the great dragon says. His wings unfold now, and the children gasp. He is even larger than they thought.

Arthur bows low to the ground. The children, not knowing what else to do, bow too. When Arthur rises, he keeps his head low. "And I am called Arthur of Fairendale," he says.

"Why are you here?" Zorag says. "Why have you crossed into my lands?"

"We had hoped for safe passage," Arthur says.

Zorag roars, and the fire escaping between his jagged teeth makes the air above them burn. "No man is allowed to cross the dragon lands."

Maude's hand squeezes Arthur's arm. Hazel squeezes his other hand. Arthur looks at the children. He did not want them to die like this. He had not supposed it would end so gruesomely. But he supposed he should have known, for the dragons had not been on friendly terms with the people for quite some time. He knew there was great risk. But they might very well have made it if the king's men had not found them.

Perhaps there is still hope. Arthur dares look at Zorag. The dragon is not looking at him or the children but stares, instead, toward the king's men.

"No man is allowed to cross the dragon lands!" Zorag roars again, and this time the whole ground shakes with the force of his growl.

Arthur hears the clatter of armor. The king's men must be shaking. He does not blame them for being afraid. He is afraid, too, though he must not let his daughter and her friends see. So he waits. He says nothing. They may be able to slip away still, for it seems as though Zorag is more interested in the king's men than he is in the children. Perhaps he will be able to strike a bargain. Perhaps they will make it after all.

Arthur removes his hand from Maude's. She looks at him. He brings one finger to his lips. The children watch, too, and no one says a single word. Arthur takes one step forward, slowly, carefully. And then another. Zorag still watches the king's men, but there are so many other dragons. The entire land stands still, except Arthur and Maude and the children, who move tiny steps forward, so small one would not even notice.

Arthur knows how little hope there is in this situation, but at least he will not die without trying.

Someone calls out from the line of king's men, "We have no quarrel with you. We only want the children."

And Zorag turns his fiery breath on Arthur and Maude and all the children, who cease to move once more. "You have brought these men to my land?" he roars.

Arthur holds up his hands higher, as if in complete surrender. "No," he says. "Please. We are only trying to protect the children. These men—" Arthur points behind him. "We must not let them take the children. We must not let the children die. We must pass through the land. Please." He is surprised to find that he is weeping.

The dragons all around begin a frightful clamor, roaring and flashing their fire and stomping the ground so the children can hardly keep their feet steady beneath them. It is as if a chorus of giant beings has joined together in an angry laugh, if you can imagine something as frightful as this. It is made more frightful still by the glowing eyes that now become slits.

The dragons, you see, are both angry and amused that humans would dare believe dragons would permit them to travel their lands, to break the sacred covenant made so many years ago, without repercussions. This is why they laugh. This is why their eyes narrow. This is why the fire becomes a heated blast, though they do not aim at the people as yet.

These dragons, led by their great and fearless chief Zorag, do not intend to let anyone go. And so it is with horror and regret that Arthur turns his face to all the wide-eyed children he has loved so deeply. They will die anyway. He has failed them. A single tear drops down Maude's face. The ground shakes beneath their feet, for the dragons are drawing closer, flanking their leader.

"It was decreed long ago," Zorag says, his neck high. His eyes flash. The children would like nothing more than to look away, but they are mesmerized by the color, the flecks of orange in yellow, as if even his eyes hold the heat that rumbles in his chest. "It was by no choice of my own, you understand." Every step is measured. This, you might imagine, makes it far more worrisome for the children, for steps measured like these most always mean danger. "We agreed that no man would cross into our lands, that we, the dragons, would not cross into the lands of men." Zorag is so close to them now they can feel the heat of his skin. "We would leave the humans to their peace, or what semblance they might conjure with their new king. And now." He drops his head so it is level with Arthur's face. His head, dear reader, is larger than Arthur's entire body, but Arthur, brave man he is, does not shrink from the dragon. Zorag stares in Arthur's eyes. Arthur stares back. "You dare defy me," the dragon says.

"We merely sought safety," Arthur says. "Protection. We did not wish to offend. There was no other way."

"There was no other way," Zorag says, "but through the dragon lands?"

"No," Arthur says. "It was the only way to protect the children. We would not have crossed if there were any other way."

Zorag roars again, this time lifting his face to the sky, and then he turns his attention upon the king's men, who remain on the perimeter of the land, no one daring to cross.

"You shall not have these people," Zorag says. The king's men do not move. "They are mine." He looks back at Arthur and Maude and the children, his eyes chilling them, though they are full of fire. "You are mine."

The children, as if they are one and the same, begin to wail.

Consolation

The king, of course, died.

King Willis married Clarion, and Cora was left to be another village girl. She felt no sadness at this, only fury. The years proved that there was not a single hope left for the villagers. There was not change coming in Fairendale. Queen Clarion was not the kind of queen Cora might have been. And this fueled the fury even more.

But there came a boy.

He was kind and tall and striking in his appearance. He was made for something more than a captain's son, and yet that is precisely what he was. He had no magic, but he loved her.

She feigned disinterest at first, for the children of the village had only ever pushed her away, aware of her differences, though not aware at all, not entirely. So when the boy showed her interest, she did not believe it, sure it was a trick. She made the loving as difficult for him as she could, teasing him, ignoring his gifts, calling attention to the difference in their age, though it was not so very much—only one year and four months, to be precise.

She had seen so much. She had kept her secret for nearly twelve years, and she could not risk anyone knowing now, after she had the king's death on her hands. If someone found out about the skin she wore at night, they would cast her out, for people in all the kingdoms were distrustful of shape shifters. And she was a blackbird, the very bird that had killed their king.

It was all of this that kept her from the boy.

Yet he continued his pursuit. He saw her for who she was. He loved her. She could tell.

So, little by little, she let him win her heart.

And then, one day, the king's army came to town with the news of his father's death, and suddenly this boy became a man and agreed to lead an army. He tried to make her understand, but she could not understand, you see. He would serve a king she was supposed to marry, a king who was no better than his father, and the hate was so large and black in her that she could do nothing but turn it on the very one she loved.

Her heart hardened.

Until one day her father came to her and said, "It is about time we found a man for you to marry."

She did not argue. She knew that this was the way of things, that when a woman reached a certain age, she would not be seen fit to marry. She could tell her father had more he wanted to say.

"The sailor who lives at the edge of the village," he said. "He is a good man. Handsome. Strong. Kind."

And so he was.

But there was someone else she loved, though the love was hard to distinguish from the hate. She wanted to marry the boy who wore armor, who made his nightly rounds in the village and lingered at her window.

But she could not forgive him for serving the king.

So she married the sailor. They had a beautiful daughter with a gift of magic that nearly paralleled her own but for the missing dark parts.

She was called Mercy.

Fire

The king's men look at their captain. Sir Greyson stares at the scene before him. Children. Dragons. Danger, all around. They will not survive a battle with the dragons. But they have been ordered, by the word of the king, to bring him the children or not return at all. And the children are there, stretched out in a line as if ready for capture, though it will not be an easy capture. They will have to ride hard, and he will lose many, perhaps even all. This he knows.

But he will also lose all if he returns to the king with this story. So he knows they must at least try.

"Prepare for battle," Sir Greyson says. His men straighten their backs, but not before a collective breath is sucked through every one of them. They did not realize they had signed up to battle dragons, you see. Many of them shake. Many of them would like nothing more than to turn on their heels and run. But they are brave men. They are loyal men. They will do what needs doing.

It is a fool's errand, at best, but Sir Greyson whispers the words again. "Prepare for battle. We must ride hard." The two men beside him whisper it to the men on their sides. And on and on down the line it goes. The men put their hands on their swords. They do not know how to fight dragons, do not even know whether swords will help them at all, but they will try. Oh, yes. They will try.

Death steps from the shadows, his black hood flapping in the wind. No one can see him, but he is, dear reader, quite a horrifying sight. He knows, you see, that this reaping will be quite easy.

Arthur turns to look behind him, just as the king's men straighten their backs, just as their hands move to the hilts of their swords, and he knows precisely what their movements mean. So he, dear brave man, turns to them. He holds up a hand. He yells to the line of men. "Stop. Please."

They remain still. Not even their horses flinch.

"Take me," he says, turning back to Zorag. "Take me instead of the children. Please. Let them go. And the king's men will get what they want, and everyone will be on their way."

"Arthur," Maude says, for she does not know the plans in Arthur's heart. She merely hears that he intends to hand them all over to the king's men, that he will not be with them to plan for what comes next. Her throat catches. She coughs, but it is more a cry than anything else. Whatever will she do without Arthur? She has never done anything of merit without Arthur. How will she survive? How will the children survive, in the hands of the king? She is not the one skilled in escape. That has always been Arthur.

Oh, Arthur. He cannot leave her.

Maude grabs his hand. He looks at her with all the love he has in his heart. They have shared many lives and many years. And she knows, by that one look of love, that he is asking the dragons in all earnestness to take him. To spare the children, so they might be captured by the king's men, the lesser of the two evils. She knows, too, that this is the only way. It is the only way they will survive.

And so she breathes, deep and long. She closes her eyes, and another single tear drops down her cheek. Arthur would give anything to wipe it away, but he must not. He must not make any movement at all, for he does not want to break the spell he may be weaving with words around the dragons.

The king's captain speaks. "No," he says. His voice carries

all the way across the great distance between them. "We must have you as well, sir. King's orders."

The dragons fill the air with their rumbles again. Zorag speaks above the noise. "The king's orders have no rule here in our lands."

The dragons glare at the king's men, and the king's men shake ever more, their armor clanking. And then one of them breaks. He is a man who has been far too long without his grieving wife, who has wondered for far too long where his little boy may be, who does not know what else to do with his desperation but move. And so he does. He charges forward, so entirely forlorn that he does not consider what his moving may unleash. And, oh, dear reader, what it will unleash.

This man gives a cry such as no one in the land has ever heard, a decidedly human cry but other-worldly as well, as if all the sorrow of all the world was confined in that one call from a soldier's mouth. It is grief that nudges the horse and races him toward the greatest danger there is in a world like Fairendale, if one were not considering the Violet Sea or the unnamed creatures of the Weeping Woods. This man does not even care that he rushes forward to his death, dear reader. Grief makes a man do strange things. Grief can turn a man reckless.

His movement throws the king's men into a frenzy. They have no idea what to do. They merely follow after him, though he is not their leader, though their leader, in fact, remains at the border, watching his men race to their deaths. He is helpless to stop them. And so it is that he, their leader, follows his men into death, a hundred paces behind.

Enough paces behind.

The world explodes in a ball of heat that burns red and orange and the deepest of blues. It burns in an unstoppable way, and it burns long and hard and hot. It consumes everything. It sets one small line of trees on fire, and so sets the entire forest ablaze. It scorches all the men and their horses, so the land is filled with horrendous screaming and the painful crying of men burning within their armor. Though, if one were to listen closely, one would hear only the cries of men and horses. No cries of a woman and children.

Where are they? How is it that they have escaped from a fire such as this one?

Maude has, in truth, underestimated herself. In the moment before the dragons loosed their fire, she urged the children to run. And so they did, Maude bringing up the rear. They ran toward a stretch of land that did not contain burning soldiers, for they knew that the dragons would be preoccupied with clearing the king's men from their lands and would not, perhaps, notice their direction. They found another cave, a smaller one, on the perimeter of the land, nearer to the forest than to Morad, and there she and the children watch the madness, watch the burning bodies and the burning woods and the burning everything. They are safe. At least they are safe.

But this is only momentary comfort, you see, for she left her dear Arthur where he was, crouching beneath the belly of the dragon Zorag. He was safe for the time being, but what will happen once the king's men are gone? What will the dragons do to Arthur?

And what will she do without him?

Maude turns away, herding the children as deep into the cave as they can possibly go. They should not look on the terror. But they have seen enough. They will remember it all their days, the way the dragons tore into the king's men and left not one of them standing. Oh, yes. One does not easily forget a horror such as that.

They will remember the voice of the massive dragon, rumbling over all the cracking and screaming and pounding: "You dare defy me. I will dare defy you."

They will remember the way it shook them in their deepest places and held them down in a cave dark and damp, damp enough to keep the fire that consumed all the land away from their bodies.

Death moves over the wreckage on silent wings.

Don't miss out on the next Fairendale adventure!

Will the dragons seek revenge for a broken treaty? Find out in
Book 5: *The Fiery Aftermath*.

Shape Shifters
A Brief History

By L.R. Patton
Author

Shape shifters have been around for hundreds of years. There are stories told about them in the ancient texts of other lands, and nearly every story book considered good education material for the children of Fairendale and the surrounding lands have stories about shape shifters.

Shape shifting is a kind of magical transformation. Shape shifters are considered those who can change into different creatures or simply adjust their size. Sometimes the shape shifters can do both, though this is not often the case.

In our earlier stories, we have established that there are six shape shifters in the land of Fairendale and those surrounding it. These six are shape shifters in the strictest definition of the term —those who can change their shape at will.

However, the dragons of Eyre, which you will meet in Book 7 of our annals, are also considered shape shifters, which means there are, in actuality, hundreds more shape shifters that have not been counted in the aging census of the land. The people in our stories do not know much about dragons, so they do not know that the dragons of Eyre have the ability to shift both size and shape.

Even later in our stories, we will meet an entire forest full of shape shifters—but these shape shifters are only permitted to change shape on a full moon. They are known as Were Creatures, and they become panthers, cougars, wolves, bears, coyotes, bats, snakes, and even creatures that have no name.

There are many reasons that shape shifters use their gifts—some of them to escape danger, some to inflict punishment on those who have wronged them. The stories of shape shifters are as unique as their abilities.

The guiding rules of shape shifters

Traditional shape shifters—those who can only change their shape—abide by many different rules, some implicit, some explicit:

The gift of shape shifting is given at birth, to a select few. It is unknown who gives this gift.

A shape shifter can only shape shift into the animal skin she is given at birth. Meaning, if one is given the gift of shape shifting into a blackbird, as Cora has been given, one can only shift into a blackbird forevermore.

A shape shifter retains her shape shifting magic even after she has borne a child. The gift of shape shifting is granted for life, though other magic, if a shape shifter possesses this gift, may fade. Or it may not.

Shape shifting is not a gift passed from parent to child. It is randomly bestowed.

A shape shifter might be a sorcerer, or he might be an ordinary person.

If a shape shifter wears his animal skin for too long, he will become the animal rather than the person. Time limits are different for every shape shifter, which means a shape shifter must know his limits.

Likewise, if a shape shifter has spent too much time between living as a human and shifting into an animal, she will lose the ability to shape shift. The gift must be practiced and used.

If a shape shifter is killed in his shape shifting form, he will return, upon death, to his ordinary, human form.

The only thing that can kill a shape shifter, if one desires to, is an arrow topped with an iron point.

How to Know If You Are a Shape Shifter

By Cora of Fairendale
Unofficial Leader of the People

Being a shape shifter is a lonely occupation. I have always been a loner, however, so this was never a worry for me. I never took much interest in the goings-on or the people in the village of Fairendale. I learned early that there was a reason I did not feel a connection with any other person. Or most other people. One excepted.

I was a shape shifter. One of the chosen.

I still do not know entirely what it means. I know that I have been given a powerful gift. I know that many do not understand shape shifters, which means that many do not understand me. It does not bother me so much, though I would very much like to know why I have been given this gift.

But the purpose of this writing is not to air my wonderings; it is to help you know if you might be a shape shifter.

Here are some clues that shape shifting might be a gift you carry:

1. You have very vivid dreams.

There were many nights before I fully developed my ability to shape shift when I thought that I was flying in the sky. They were the most wonderful dreams, for what child does not want to fly? These dreams were different from other dreams in their vivid reality. I could not tell that they were dreams at all.

2. You lose moments of time.

Sometimes, when I was a young girl, I would find that I had been lost to the world for whole hours at a time. I could not remember a single thing that had happened during that time. I later learned that this was because my animal skin had crept up on me unexpectedly, and I had spent the last several hours as a blackbird, unbeknownst to me.

3. Your limbs turn into random animal parts.

There were strange and disturbing instances when I would be sweeping my father's cottage and my fingers would suddenly become feathers. Sometimes my legs would shorten unexplainably. Other times my mouth would become a sharp and pointed beak. Sometimes, instead of singing while I completed all the chores, my voice would emerge as the squawk of a blackbird.

I did not tell my father, for fear that he might believe me mad.

The skill of shifting your skin must be meticulously developed over a number of years, so it is worthwhile to know if you are a shape shifter earlier rather than later. Perhaps these tips will help you determine whether you have this ability.

And if you are a shape shifter, here is how to shift into your unique shape:

Close your eyes and imagine that you are the animal you have been dreaming about. Open your eyes and enjoy.

7 Ways Dragons Differ From Humans

By Your Narrator
Storyteller

In the land of Fairendale, dragons are largely unknown and misunderstood. The people of Fairendale know of them, of course, but they do not trust them, and this has kept them from discovering what is unique and amazing about dragons. Little is known about them, in fact.

Most of the people in the Fairendale stories do not know, for example, that some of the dragons in their land can blend in with their surroundings, much like chameleons. These particular dragons also have a shape-shifting ability of sorts, though they never become anything less than a dragon. But they can shift from very small dragons to very large dragons. (You will meet these dragons in Book 7.)

Some of the dragons in the realm form what looks like large mountains and breathe red-hot fire lava from their bellies, and people call them Fire Mountains, thinking that is what they are. It is not. The mountains are dragons, and they are very, very good at hiding. (You will meet these dragons in Book 12.)

Some dragons roam the skies, luring their prey in with their beauty, while others prefer land, especially when food is plentiful. Some of them are quite content to live as far as possible from any humans, and some of them seek out humans for company—or food. Some of them are vicious, others docile.

Dragons differ greatly from humans, of course. Here are

seven of the many ways they are different:

1. Dragons engage in a Long Sleep.

Dragons enter what is called a Long Sleep when their inherent alert systems tell them that danger is not present. The closest thing the human and animal world has to the Long Sleep is hibernation. But during the Long Sleep, a dragon essentially fades from the land, becoming rocks or boulders or, yes, mountains. Their hearts only beat one time every day, which is why they can no longer be detected with a human eye.

While one might argue that you would notice the thump of a dragon's heart—for it shakes the whole ground—when a thousand of them are gathered together in the same land, it is also true that when many dragons enter the Long Sleep near each other, their bodies become nearly one. Their heartbeats become one. This means that only once per day does the land around them give a violent, shivering rumble. Many do not even know they live near a dragon at all because of this.

A dragon easily enters the Long Sleep. He simply has to curl up and close his eyes. A dragon is also easily woken from the Long Sleep, for while his body shuts down, his senses remain ever alert. Dragons can feel the softest of footsteps, and they will shake him awake, possibly annoying him in the process.

Some dragons sleep while they guard hordes of treasure, like those in Fairendale's northernmost land, Guardia. Some sleep in deserted lands, like those in Ashvale, which is said to be a land of Fire Mountains (but we know is not). Some sleep because there is nothing else to do, as the dragons of Morad did for many years.

If or when a dragon is woken from the Long Sleep, his heart begins to beat at a pace of about one thump every five minutes. If a human heart beat once every five minutes, that human would be dead. Or very nearly.

2. Dragons walk on four feet and fly.

This is a more obvious difference, of course. But I did not want to leave it out simply because it is obvious. I know some children who have tried to fly like dragons—some from rooftops, some from trampolines, some from the tops of their mother's car, so I feel it important to underline: Humans have two legs and they cannot fly. Please stop trying.

A dragon in flight is a majestic sight. One can watch it, mesmerized, for entire minutes before one realizes one should probably begin running for dear life, particularly from the Black Dragons of Daron Valley in the south, who are quite vicious to behold and the most dangerous of all the dragons, with the exception of their counterparts, the White Dragons of Werizod in the north.

The Black Dragons of Daron Valley reside near the land of Lincastle and like nothing more than to find a single solitary figure on the beach, which they will then snap up into their powerful jaws and carry into the sky, never to be seen again. That is the only time a human will be able to fly, after which point he or she will die a gruesome death. I shall spare you the details.

So if ever you are on a beach and see flying above you a dragon with black scales that shimmer and sparkle in the sun, turning every color of the rainbow, run as fast as you can.

3. Dragons live for hundreds of years.

Some dragons can live five hundred or six hundred years. In fact, a dragon of one hundred is considered a young dragon. Zorag, who rules the lands of Morad, is a dragon of one hundred forty-two years, which is still quite young by the standards of a dragon. Though he would say he has lived many lifetimes in his sorrow.

A human, on the other hand, has, at most, a little more than one hundred years allotted them, if they care well for their mind, body, and spirit. Have you played outside today?

4. Dragons breathe fire.

It is true that some humans—such as parents—can breathe what seems like fire every now and again, but despite what their children may think, no human is able to breathe actual fire. Dragons, on the other hand, breathe fire hot enough to disintegrate any piece of a person who ventures too close.

All the dragons in our story have a telltale sign that they are about to erupt with fire: their necks heat up to a beautiful glowing red color, and if one is not too enamored by the sparkle of it, one would do well to skedaddle so as not to melt upon contact with a dragon's breath.

5. Dragons use their tails for balance.

Humans, of course, do not have tails. We use our big toes for balance.

The tails of dragons, however, are not simply used for balance. They serve a variety of purposes. Dragons use their tails to eliminate their enemies, to steer them in flight (like a rudder of sorts), to curl around them while they sleep, to secure a human (much like a python snake), to knock their prey to the ground, to thump the ground in order to ensure silence, and to aid them in climbing tall cliffs and mountains.

A tail can be used for many things. Sometimes I wish I had one.

6. Dragons have more teeth than humans—and eat raw meat because of it.

If we ate raw meat, we would quickly wish we had not. Humans who eat raw meat, especially the red kind, become sickened to a point where we might feel we are dying (we are likely not). Perhaps more notable, however, is the fact that we have only thirty-two teeth, and they are not the sort of teeth that can easily rip and chew raw meat. Dragons, on the other hand, have a whole mouth of one hundred twenty-six teeth, all of them razor sharp and ready to rip.

(For the more curious among you, the teeth of dragons are not blackened on the side that cannot be seen by observers. They are golden. How is it I know, you ask? Well, in a moment of foolishness, I once placed by head in the mouth of a dragon so I could make my notes. You should never, ever try it yourself.)

7. Dragons have scales.

During the coldest days of winter, our skin might possibly contain patches that resemble scales, but I assure you, those patches are not scales. They are only bits of dead skin.

Our skin does much of what a dragon's scales do. A dragon's scales encapsulate their body temperature, helping them regulate it through cold days and hot days alike. Dragons, of course, are cold blooded (which you might also note is a difference between humans and dragons—we are warm-blooded), and the scales are necessary for inner warmth.

Scales also help dragons move on the ground. They slide back and forth when they are walking on four feet, almost like waddling reptiles. Can you imagine the sound a waddling dragon makes? It is something like a cross between your baby brother shaking a maraca and a thousand librarians shushing you.

Dragons also use their scales for protection, water retention, and camouflage.

Dragons are quite beautiful creatures, dangerous and mysterious. Great for observing from a distance. But beware, dear reader, of venturing too close.

The Royal Family of Fairendale

King Willis: The current king of Fairendale. Has a deep love for sweet rolls, and it shows in his, well, wideness.

Queen Clarion: The current queen of Fairendale. Is underestimated by her husband, but we shall see just how powerful she is soon enough.

Prince Virgil: Son of King Willis and Queen Clarion, best friend of Theo. Prefers rye bread with melted butter to sweet rolls, depending on the day.

King Sebastien: Deceased king of Fairendale, exception to the line of boys who tried to steal thrones and were, upon failing at their quest, forever banished to sail the Violet Sea. Was killed by a blackbird.

The Villagers of Fairendale

Arthur: Village furniture maker and magic instructor to girls who possess the gift of magic. Is a bit reckless but always manages to come out on the other side—though one is not always assured it will be so.

Maude: Arthur's wife. Bakes spectacular pumpkin sugar cookies. Prefers caution to reckless abandon.

Hazel: Daughter of Arthur and Maude, twin of Theo. Cares for the village sheep and can even, amazingly, understand them.

Theo: Son of Arthur and Maude, twin of Hazel. Finishes his chores early so he can sit in on magic lessons.

Mercy: Daughter of Cora, best friend of Hazel. Prefers spectacular acts of magic to "boring" ones.

Cora: Mother of Mercy, widow, shape shifter. A woman who moves.

Garron: The town gardener. Talks to plants as though they can hear him. Has three sons: 12-year-old twins and a 13-year-old.

Bertie: The town baker. Enjoys showing off his air-kneading skills for the children.

Staff of Fairendale Castle

Garth: Page for King Willis, the oldest of twelve children. Sometimes calls King Willis "Your Wideness."

Cook: One of the few shape shifters in the land. Shape shifts into a bear. Is highly annoyed by her assistant, Calvin.

Calvin: An orphan who began working as Cook's assistant instead of traveling to live with distant relatives in Ashvale—and so did not perish in the Fire Mountain that claimed the entire population of Ashvale many years ago. Tasked with feeding the prisoners in the dungeons beneath the dungeons.

Sir Greyson: Captain of the king's guard. Receives medicine, which keeps his mother alive, in exchange for his service to the king. Carries a magical sword that cannot be lifted by any but him.

Sir Merrick: Second in command to Sir Greyson.

Important Prophets

Aleen: A prophetess who is one hundred forty-two years old, from the kingdom of White Wind. Wears ebony skin and what appears to be a collection of snakes for hair (though it is not).

Yerin: A prophet who is one hundred forty-two years old, from the wild woodland between Lincastle and Eastermoor. Has white hair that makes the dark of the dungeons where he is imprisoned a bit less dark.

Dragons of Morad

Zorag: King of the dragons of Morad. Lost his parents in the Great Battle, when King Sebastien stole the throne from the Good King Brendon. Would like nothing more than peace.

Blindell: Zorag's cousin, raised as the dragon king's son. Lost his parents in the Great Battle, when King Sebastien stole the throne from the Good King Brendon. Would like nothing more than revenge.

Larus: One of the elder dragons of Morad, male. Counselor to Zorag.

Malera: One of the elder dragons of Morad, female.

Counselor to Zorag.

The lost 12-year-old children of Fairendale

Ursula

Chester

Charles

Thumbelina (known as Lina among the children)

Minnie

Jasper

Frederick

Ruby

Martin

Oscar

Homer

Anna

Aurora

Rose

Edgar

Harriet (known as Hattie among the children)

Isabel (known as Izzy among the children)

Ralph

Dorothy

Julian

Tom Thumb

Philip

About the Author

While she has never possessed the gift of magic, L.R.'s teachers claimed she had a gift for words, which one might agree is quite like a gift of magic. Bringing a story to life that did not exist before is very much like transforming an old shoe into a dish towel. L.R. feels quite honored that she was given this gift and hopes to use it to encourage other young writers to discover their own gifts, for what is the world without words and stories?

L.R. is the queen of her castle in San Antonio, TX. She lives with her king and her six young princes, who daily give her inspiration for more grand tales of magic and adventure.

www.lrpatton.com

A Note From L.R.

I hope you've enjoyed reading this book from the annals of Fairendale's history. The world of Fairendale has been a lovely world to create, and I've had fun sketching maps, re-reading fairy tales and thinking, endlessly, about characters and their plights—because a series like this one takes lots and lots of time and hard work. But because it's always been my dream to create a fantasy world and share it with my readers, I knew it was something I had to do. (So, you see, dreams really do come true.)

If you have any questions about Fairendale or simply want to send me a note to tell me who your favorite character is or what kinds of extras you'd like to see me release in the future (a *Creatures of the Violet Sea* is coming soon!), email me at lr@lrpatton.com. I always enjoy hearing from my young readers.

Please consider leaving (or ask your parent to leave) a review of this book wherever you bought it. Reviews help get books into the hands of potential new readers, which is incredibly important for authors like me. And don't forget to pick up your free bonus materials when you stop by my web site! (www.lrpatton.com)

Thank you so much for supporting my work.

In love,

L.R.

Enjoy more stories from the magical Fairendale series:

LRPatton.com/Fairendale

Starter Library

Once upon a time...

The kingdom of Fairendale used to be the most peaceful in all the lands. Its people had never held a weapon before. And now they must, for the sake of the land. For the sake of their families. For the sake of their beloved king.

Read all about the king who had no heir, the girl who had magic, the dragon they loved, and the battle that changed everything in Fairendale's short story prequel, "The Good King's Fall."

Get it FREE, along with bonus materials "The Magical Rules of Fairendale" and "The Lands of Fairendale," for a limited time.

To get your FREE bonus materials, visit *
LRPatton.com/goodking

*Must be 13 or older to be eligible